I0596499

Skylab 5

by Bill Bogen

Chapter 1: First Contact

April, 1969

Ted put the bomb on a table in the Undergraduate Library. It was his first and he was anxious to see how well it performed. The seven sticks of dynamite were in a duffel bag, hooked up to a battery and a wind-up kitchen timer. Students passed by as he reached into the bag, turned the timer to ten minutes, and set a switch to the armed position. Ted slowly withdrew his hand. He was committed now and felt liberated. In this simple act, he was separating himself from the disgusting swarms of humanity who were raping the Earth for resources and destroying the planet with pollution. It was the beginning of a heroic journey. He turned and strode out of the library.

#

Harry Remains sat at a table in the UGLi, trying to study tort law. It was a beautiful spring day in Ann Arbor and the Diag was crowded with student groups protesting the War in Vietnam. He'd rather be out there with them instead of slogging through dry legal texts. He was finishing his last year in his JD program but he preferred hanging out in the Undergraduate Library rather than the Law School. He distracted himself by watching other students. Some guy fussed with a bag on a table then slowly pulled his hand from it, left the bag, and walked to an exit. *That's weird behavior*, Harry thought. He stood up, stretched, and walked over to the bag. It was sitting open. He didn't touch it because he didn't want to be accused of stealing someone's stuff. He leaned over and peeked inside. *Holy shit.* He suddenly felt faint and his vision narrowed. He took a deep breath. Then he walked quickly to a fire alarm switch on the wall and pulled it. The clanging bell was distant but echoed through the library loudly enough to bring everyone's heads up from their studies.

Harry jumped onto a table and shouted, "This is not a drill. There is a bomb on this floor. Walk, don't run, for the exit."

He figured if people didn't see a fire, they might ignore the alarm. But with the radical anti-war Weatherman group attacking Federal buildings, a bomb seemed a believable threat. The library quickly cleared. Harry was leaving too but saw a big blond guy headed for the bag. *Christ, some idiot trying to be a hero.*

"Stop!" Harry shouted, as he ran back toward the bomb.

The guy calmly leaned over the bag and reached inside. Time froze for Harry as he skidded to a stop, closed his eyes, and waited for the blast. He wondered if it would hurt. Would he even hear it before he died? After a few more such deep thoughts, he realized nothing had happened. He opened one eye and saw the guy looking at him with an amused expression.

"It's OK. I pulled out the blasting cap." He held up a small cylinder then lay it on the table.

Harry let out the breath he had been holding and said, "Why don't we step outside and wait for the cops and firemen?"

"Why not just leave?"

"Because," Harry said, "the bomb squad might appreciate knowing what they're getting into and the cops might like a description of the guy who left the bomb. Also, you just left fingerprints on the blasting cap. Wouldn't you rather be a hero than a suspect?"

The fire alarm stopped. The Fire Department must have arrived and shut it off.

"All good points," the guy said, as he stuck out his hand. "I'm Luke."

"Harry."

They shook hands.

The kitchen timer buzzed loudly. Harry jumped. Luke just grinned.

"You knew that was going to happen, didn't you?" said Harry accusingly.

"Yeah."

"You've got a sick sense of humor, man."

As they headed for the exit, Harry said, "I have an idea, if you're willing to play a part. But we have to act fast."

Luke listened and nodded. They split up as they left the building. Harry circled behind a crowd of gawking students. He saw Luke step around a fire truck and head toward two cops getting out of a patrol car. As Harry searched for the bomber, he kept one eye on Luke who was putting on a dramatic performance for the police, telling them about the bomb but also waving his arms about as if telling an epic adventure tale to kids around a campfire. *Christ man*, Harry thought, *don't lay it on too thick. or the cops will think you're high on something.*

Harry recognized the bomber. He was staring at Luke while students milled about. Harry walked up behind him. *If I were a bomber, would I carry a gun?* Harry put two fingers to his lips and blew a piercing whistle. The bomber clapped his hands over his ears and turn around to glare at him. Then reached into a jacket pocket. *Oh shit, this one does. Don't freeze, don't freeze, don't freeze.* Harry froze. He saw the bomber rise up off the ground and then come crashing down. Harry watched Luke pin the bomber down as cops ran up.

He took a deep breath of relief. "Officers, this is the guy who set the bomb. I saw him place it. I figured he would wait around to see the results and also that he would be fascinated by my friend's discussion with you. So I searched through the spectators until I found him."

The bomber was taken away cursing. Harry directed some cops to the bomb. Others took Luke and Harry to Police Headquarters to get their statements.

#

"Full names?" asked the detective.

"Luke L Priss."

"What's the 'L' stand for?"

"Nothing. It's just 'L', like the 'S' in Harry S Truman doesn't stand for anything. It's kind of an inside family joke."

The detective was not amused. He stared at Luke then turned to Harry.

"Harold Remains, but you can call me Harry. No middle initial."

The detective gave long-haired Harry the fisheye. He looked like he thought it might have been Harry who planted the bomb. He slowly wrote down every detail of the bomb scene, where they were sitting, their view of the duffel bag, and a description of the suspect. It was late afternoon before they were done and back on campus.

Luke checked his watch. "5:20. So I missed three classes for that."

"Yeah, me too," said Harry, "I still think it was the right thing to do, though. Hey, I'm meeting a friend at Dominick's. Why don't you join us? I'll buy."

After Harry ordered pizza at the counter, they took their drinks and sat at a table inside, with Luke facing the entrance. Harry noted the funny looks they got from other customers. *Yeah, he thought, hippies and jocks don't usually hang out together, do we?* Luke was muscular, six foot two, eyes of blue, blonde hair cropped in a short flat-top. He wore a button down shirt and khakis. Harry was of average build and had shoulder-length curly black hair and dark eyes. He was in bell-bottom jeans and wore a black tee shirt emblazoned with a picture of the spiral Milky Way galaxy. An arrow pointing to one star was labeled 'You Are Here'. They each took the measure of the other in silence for a few seconds.

"ROTC?" Harry said.

"No, I just like my hair short," said Luke.

"Quite the rebel. So why did you defuse that bomb instead of just leaving? It could have killed
you."

Luke shrugged. "I've worked with dynamite before, back on the farm in Kansas blowing up tree stumps and such. If I had let it explode, the Library would be closed for weeks. I didn't want my research interrupted."

"Research? What kind of research are you doing?"

"Nothing toward my Masters degree, just personal. I'm interested in rocketry and I was looking into the history of space projects. The UGLi has some good books on that."

Harry's eyes widened. "Rocketry? Why? Do you want to be an astronaut?"

"Well, sort of," Luke said, "I hope to design spaceships, maybe pilot them, but probably not for NASA."

"Why not NASA? Aren't they the only game in town?"

Luke was about to answer but his eyes became fixed on the entrance.

Ah, thought Harry, seeing Luke's face, *that must be Althea.*

Amused, he watched Luke's quickly changing reactions. Awed. Surprised and pleased that she was headed toward their table. Sitting straighter. Putting on a carefully neutral face.

Without turning, Harry moved to make a space for her.

"Hey Althea, this is Luke. We caught a mad bomber. Well, at least he was mad after we caught him."

Althea was dark brown, lean, and almost as tall as Luke. Her high cheekbones, perfect skin, and short afro often led those meeting her to think she was a model from Ethiopia rather than a medical student from Detroit. Althea leaned over and gave her friend Harry a peck on the cheek.

She didn't usually greet him that way and he suspected she was sending some sort of message to Luke. Harry had no idea what the message was but he wasn't complaining.

"Hello Luke," Althea said. "Any friend of Harry's...".

"Wonderful," Luke breathed. Then, flushed, "I mean, it's a pleasure to meet you, Althea."

"I just heard about the bomb scare in the UGLi," she said, "What did you two have to do with that?"

Harry told her the story and generously embellished Luke's role in it.

"Weren't you afraid to confront someone willing to kill random students?" she asked.

Luke and Harry stared at her.

She smiled, "Now the thought occurs to you."

Luke said, "I guess I assumed he was a bomber, not a shooter, and his bomb was in the UGLi."

Harry added, "Well, it turned out he did have a gun. But if we did nothing, he'd just go plant another bomb somewhere else so…". He shrugged.

"Do you think he was a Weatherman?" asked Althea.

"Don't know," said Harry.

Luke said, "I don't think so. The Weathermen bomb Federal buildings to protest the war but they give warnings and don't seem to actually want to kill anyone. Our bomber left his in a crowded space. I think he was a loner nut."

They sat in silence for a bit.

"So Luke was about to tell me why he wants to be a rocket jockey but not for NASA," Harry said.

Luke flushed but Althea gave him a serious look.

"Why not NASA, Luke? You're not planning to be a cosmonaut, are you?".

"No, and after I get out of the Air National Guard maybe NASA will have ships I can fly. It's just that, after we land on the Moon, I expect the Space Program to start winding down. Private space travel might be all I can hope for."

"Are you kidding?" Harry said, "The government is spending billions on the Apollo Program. How could they let it all end?"

"Billions, yes, but how are they spending it?"

"What do you mean?" asked Althea.

"Well, they could do the first landing this summer exactly as planned. Get two guys on the Moon before the Russians do. I see the political sense
in that."

"And then? What would you do if you were in charge?" Althea asked.

Harry saw from her expression that her question was serious, not mocking.

"I would have taken some time to also design unmanned cargo ships," Luke said. "Send one to the Moon before each manned landing to deliver shelters and supplies. That would actually have made the missions safer."

"So astronauts could wait for rescue if something went wrong." Althea said.

"Exactly. Also, our crews could stay on the Moon for months doing research instead of just a few days. Make it a permanent moon-base with scientists from lots of countries visiting, like an Antarctic base. Imagine the world-wide positive political impact of that! But instead, it's just a race, the Space Race. And what happens when you win a race? You take your medal and go home."

Harry said,"So young to be so cynical! What about the

Integrated Program Plan NASA is working on? Space tugs, stations around the Earth and Moon, nuclear rockets,..."

Althea added,"And trips to Mars!"

Luke said, "A nice wish list but Congress will never fund it. I doubt if they would have funded my version of Apollo. And how do you two know about such things? What are you studying?"

Harry said,"I've got an MBA and wrapping up a law degree. Then it's back to Vegas to help run the family business."

Althea said, "And I'm finishing my medical degree this term then starting my residency in Detroit."

Luke said, "Wow to both. I'm impressed. I'm just going to be a simple itinerant engineer. Got a BS in Mechanical Engineering and now one year to go for my Masters in Aerospace. OK, so why do you two have an interest in space?"

Althea said, "Harry and I met at a World Science Fiction Convention in Cleveland. Turned out we both went to U of M and both loved Robert Heinlein's stories."

"Like 'The Moon is a Hard Mattress'," Harry said.

Althea elbowed him and said, "And other authors too. So being into science fiction lead to an interest in space travel."

Luke said, "I love science fiction too. My uncle gave me all his old *Astounding* and *Galaxy* magazines when I was a kid. But I've never been to a science fiction convention," as he looked steadily at Althea.

Harry smiled. *Nice move..*

Althea said, "Oh, you should come to one. The next World Con is this summer in Saint Louis."

Luke said, "That sounds great."

Althea and Luke gazed silently at each other. Harry heard his name called.

"Ah, our pizza's ready. I'll be right back."

Althea said,"Oh, sorry Harry, I can't stay. I have to meet one of my professors. Gotta go."

Luke jumped up. "May I walk with you?"

Althea smiled and Harry thought, *Oh yeah, this is going places*.

Harry said, "That's fine, you guys go on without me. I like pizza so very much. Maybe I'll see you two again sometime soon."

But they were already gone. Harry sighed, got his order, and ate a slice. He noticed some students at a nearby table. He'd seen them at demonstrations and knew they were Weathermen members. He dropped the rest of the pizza on their table as he left and said,"Here you go guys. Viva La Revolución."

#

Althea and Luke walked along the Diag.

"So Luke, where are you from?"

"Kansas, born and raised on a little farm. You?"

"Detroit. I think I drove by a farm once."

Luke nodded. "That's good. It's nice that we have something in common." They walked in silence for a bit.

Finally Luke asked, "So are you and Harry…?" He hesitated.

"What?"

"Together? An item? A couple? In a committed relationship? Eternal soul mates? I'm trying to be discreet here."

She laughed. "No, just very good friends."

Luke looked relieved. They entered a building and stopped outside her professor's office.

"Nice to meet you, Luke. Maybe I'll see you again sometime."

"How about tonight?"

She faced him with raised eyebrows and a small smile.

"I mean, we both missed out on free pizza. Can I have dinner with you tonight?"

She was about to answer him when a young black couple passed them. They glared at Luke, the big white jock hitting on a black girl. Then an older white couple walked by. They stared disapprovingly at the negro girl coming on to the nice-looking white boy.

Luke and Althea watched the couples silently, then faced each other.

Luke said, "Well, the people have spoken. And what do you say, Althea?"

She smiled as she opened the door . "Chinese food would be nice. Can you wait for me?"

"As long as it takes."

Chapter 2: Future History

Althea and Luke lay in bed in her apartment. Sunlight filled the room. "I hate school," she said.

Luke laughed. "No, you don't. You love it. It's just that we'd rather be together than taking final exams."

Althea rolled toward him, lay her head on his chest, and said,"Luke, what are we going to do?"

"Get dressed and go to class?"

"You know what I mean."

Luke pressed his hand on the beautiful small of her beautiful back, kissed her, and said, "OK, I've got a plan. It's crazy but it just might work. You graduate with honors and move to Detroit, live with your parents, and finish your residency in three years."

He kissed her again and continued, "I graduate in a year. I hope. Then I move to Nebraska and spend a year at Air National Guard Flight School. Then I try to get posted near you. You get hired by a most prestigious hospital. I get hired to be a pilot for Crashlandia Airlines or something or other, while I figure out how to become an astronaut. Somewhere in there, we get married."

Althea stared at him. "Boy, we've known each other for twelve days. You don't waste any time."

"Why should I?," said Luke, as he got out of bed. "Life is short. I've always trusted my own judgment. And as soon as I kissed you, I knew I could love you for the rest of my life. You fit with me."

"I complete you?" she said wryly. Luke was getting dressed.

He said, "I may be a romantic but I'm not an idiot. You could live your life perfectly well without me and I could probably limp along in a gray, sad existence without you. But everything feels richer and brighter when I'm with you and I want to keep that feeling going forever."

Althea got out of bed and stretched while Luke watched with great appreciation and gratitude.

She said softly, "Are you proposing to me?"

"No."

She raised her eyebrows.

Luke said, "You don't have my certainty about us. You're going to need some time to decide about me, I think. I can wait until you're ready to love me or leave me."

She hugged him and said, "Then I agree with your plan." His eyes lit up.

"Except for the 'somewhere in there we get married' part." His face fell.

"Cool your jets!" She laughed. "Let's go slowly, OK? Go with me to the World Con this summer. After that I'll be super busy with my residency. Who knows how often we'll be able to see each other? Let's see how we feel in a year or two." She kissed him. Then swatted his butt.

"OK flyboy," she said, "Off to finals. Try not to fail."

"Yes'm."

Chapter 3: Stranger in a Strange Land

April 2, 1972

Luke peered through the window of the taxi. "Pull over here." The streets around Eastern Market in Detroit were crowded with shoppers and vendors. The Lion of Judah restaurant had been hard to find. The building was narrow and long, with the family apartment above. He stood outside and hesitated. He had not seen Althea in months. Her residency in Detroit and his assignment at the airbase in Nevada limited their relationship mostly to letters and phone calls, with a rare visit. He missed her deeply. She had finally agreed that he could meet her parents. He took a short leave, booked a room at the David Whitney Hotel in Detroit, and landed on the third anniversary of their first meeting at Dominick's in Ann Arbor. *Restaurants seem to play a big role in our lives.* He patted the small box in his jacket pocket. *Here's hoping I'm as lucky now as I was then.* He joined the crowd inside.

\#

Abeba worked the cash register and waited tables while her husband Kofi prepared the meals in the small kitchen in the back of the narrow building. *What a day for both waiters to call in sick,* she thought. *Althea's young man is going to get a terrible impression of us.* Lunchtime was always busy but the slow service was making for cranky customers. She saw the large blond man walk in, conspicuous in a sea of black customers. *My, he is a good-looking white boy.* He worked his way toward her, apologizing to customers as he squeezed past.

"Missus Nespla?" She nodded.

He bowed slightly. "I'm Luke. Looks like I caught you at a bad, well, a busy time."

She spread her hands and smiled ruefully. "Short-staffed today. And I'm sorry but Althea will be late."

"Can I help?" he offered, "I waited tables in college."

"Oh, I couldn't ask you…." but he had already hung up his

jacket near the register and rolled up his sleeves. He turned and starting bussing tables, clearing away dirty dishes. Customers looked up at him, startled. He carried an armload of plates back toward the kitchen.

#

Kofi worked furiously at the stove preparing lunch orders, next to the big sink stacked with dirty dishes. A tall white guy appeared with even more.

"Who the hell are you?" Kofi said.

"Luke Priss, sir. Glad to meet you. Shall I start washing or carry out some orders?"

"Uh, orders. We have enough clean dishes to get through lunch." Kofi pointed at a tray full of food. "Table five."

"Fifth table from the front?"

"Yes, yes." Luke left with the food.

What the hell, thought Kofi.

Abeba was taking a lunch order from old Missus Bidwell when Luke came and filled her water glass. The cranky old lady eyed him skeptically. "Boy, where you come from? I ain't never seen you here before."

"Kansas, ma'am. We don't have any African restaurants there and I heard this was the best. So here I am." She laughed.

The lunch crowd finally dissipated and there were no customers at the moment. It was close to two o'clock, when they normally stopped serving lunch, so Abeba chose to lock the front door and hang out the 'Closed' sign. She found Luke in the kitchen washing dishes. Kofi was still cooking.

"Luke, stop!" Abeba said. "Kofi, what are you doing, letting him wash dishes?"

Kofi protested, "He insisted."

"Well, come out front, the two of you."

"Let me finish making lunch for us first."

Luke put his jacket on. He and Abeba went to a booth.

"Thank you Luke. That was really not necessary for you to do."

"My pleasure, ma'am. Thanks for letting me help out."

"Althea should be here soon," she said, "And happy to see you."

A calico cat appeared at Luke's feet. He reached a hand down to her.

"Hey honey, who are you?" The cat skittered away.

"That's Belkis. She disappears around strangers. You should feel honored to even see her." Luke kept his hand in place.

The cat happened to pass the booth again and paused to sniff the back of Luke's hand. He was silent and didn't move. Abeba let the conversation pause and watched Luke. He didn't try to grab or pet Belkis. The cat strolled away. She returned a few more times and eventually rubbed her face against the back of his hand. He gently pushed against her. She leaned in.

Abeba said, "Yes, she can take a while to trust someone. But I see that you are patient."

They heard a key in the front door. Althea stepped in. "Mama, why are you closed early?"

Luke rose from his seat and turned to her. Abeba watched Althea's face closely. She saw pleasure and affection. And something else. *Caution?* The two hugged. After a beat, Abeba saw Althea relax into his arms. *They're almost the same height,* Abeba thought. Althea had been a gangly, shy, and awkward teenager and was still self-conscious about her height, which she got from her father. But she had grown into a dark, lean, striking woman and Abeba thought the two made a beautiful couple. *What will my grandchildren look like?* They sat down in the booth. At that moment Kofi came out of the kitchen with a big platter of food. Abeba saw his expression stiffen at seeing Luke and Althea together.

Abeba said, "Althea dear, I closed up a bit early so we could eat and talk undisturbed. We'd like to get to know Luke better."

Kofi snorted. "Or know him at all. You've told me nothing about him, Althea. Have you shared with your Mother perhaps? What is he to you? Are you ashamed of him?"

"Kofi!" Abeba said. She could see Althea was about to make an angry retort but Luke spoke first.

"Mister Nespla, those are good questions. I'd like to hear

the answers too. You and Missus Nespla can, of course, ask me anything you like." He looked at the platter of lamb, beef, lentil, and vegetable dishes.. There were no knives or forks on the table. "So I tear off a piece of flatbread and use that to scoop up the food, yes?" He began to eat. "This is delicious." The three Nesplas stared at him.

Luke continued, "Althea, I have to say that you haven't shared much with me about your family either. Which is your right, of course. But I think you let me visit today so we could get to know each other. May I ask some questions too?"

Althea leaned back in her seat. "Why not? Sure, let's have a free-for-all!" she said sarcastically as she glared at her father.

Abeba held up her hands. "No. We are eating together. We will have a peaceful conversation." She took a salt shaker and held it up. "A new rule: whoever holds this may ask one question. When they have been answered, they will pass the truth-shaker to someone else. Kofi, please start." She handed him the shaker.

"This is ridicu--".

"Kofi."

"All right. Fine." He grasped the shaker like a judge's gavel. "Luke Priss, what are your intentions toward my daughter?"

"I hope she will someday marry me."

Abeba saw a mixture of joy and confusion pass over Althea's face. Kofi held up a finger, taking a deep breath for a comment but Abeba interrupted. "There's your answer. Pass me the truth-shaker." He snorted but handed it to her.

"Luke, what kind of name is Priss?" she asked.

"Mama!" said Althea. Abeba shrugged.

"Originally French but my folks came from Scotland. It meant 'excellent, noble, highly valued'." Luke gestured at himself. "Of course." The women laughed. Luke took the truth-shaker. He looked at Kofi.

"And what about your surname, Mister Nespla?" Kofi looked embarrassed but Abeba laughed.

"Let me answer that," she said. Kofi sighed and rolled his eyes.

"It comes from the distant past, 1944," she said.

Luke cocked his head. "1944 BC?"

She laughed. "No, just twenty eight years ago." She leaned forward conspiratorially.

"World War 2 was still raging in the world. Mussolini's army had invaded Ethiopia years before and killed hundreds of Orthodox Christians like us, with the blessing of Pope Pius XI and the silence of his successor, Pius XII. It took years to drive all the Italians out." She put a hand on her husband's arm. "My Kofi was one of the brave guerillas who fought the invaders."

Kofi smiled and patted her hand. "Yes," he said, "but not all Catholics are bad. We had a friend who had emigrated to Michigan and worked for Bishop Magner, up in Marquette." He gestured at the framed photo hanging over the booth of a man in priestly garb. "The Bishop, may he rest in peace, rejected the fascist policies of his Popes. He sponsored us to enter the United States."

Abeda said, "I was very pregnant when we arrived at Ellis Island. We so much wanted Althea to be born in a land of peace and freedom. When the
Immigration officer took our passports, I was so scared! He stared at my big belly. Very rude!"

She put on a deep gruff voice. "'Why do you have different surnames? Are you not married?"

Kofi said angrily. "I showed him a copy of our marriage license. I told him that Ethiopians do not usually have surnames. We often use our father's given name as such. So my wife and I had different names."

"That won't do," said Abeda sternly as the mock-Immigration officer. She went on in her own voice. "I saw the man's name tag said 'LeCroix'. I was so exhausted that I foolishly thought he must be French. So, with the little French I knew, I said 'It is possible for you to assign us a name, n'est-ce pas?' He answered, 'Fine. 'Nespla' it is.', wrote that on the entry form, and stamped our passports."

Kofi snorted and said "The man was an idiot." Abeba squeezed Kofi's arm.

"I didn't care. I saluted and said 'Merci, officer!' And that is how the Nespla family came to America"

Luke laughed. "That was great!" He pointed at the other

picture on the wall above the booth, one of a bearded man in an elaborate uniform.

"I see you honor Emperor Haile Selassie as well."

"Yes," said Abeba, "We would not be here if it weren't for the two of them."

Luke tilted his head quizzically and was about to ask another question when he realized he still held the truth-shaker.

"Oh, sorry. Whose turn is it?"

The Nesplas were suddenly quiet and reserved. They had stopped eating. Luke looked at each of them.

"I'm sorry," he said again, "Is something wrong?" Althea looked at her father then her mother.

"Mama, Papa, may I?" They nodded somberly. "Go ahead and ask your question Luke, it's OK."

Luke looked confused. "I don't want to upset…"

"It's OK," she repeated.

Luke put the truth-shaker in the middle of the table.

"All right. Althea, how did the Emperor help bring your family here?"

"He ended slavery in Ethiopia in 1942."

Luke stared at her. "What? Slavery? How?"

"Ethiopia had been a slave state for centuries," she said, "My ancestors were free but there was a famine and they chose to sell their children into slavery rather than watch them starve." Kofi clenched a fist and stared silently down at the table.

"I'm sorry Papa. Luke should know." Kofi nodded.

"My father was trained to be a cook, my mother a maid. She was lucky to be dark or 'tigur' as they called it. A light-skinned girl as pretty as she was might be raped and trained to be a concubine for some rich bastard."

"Jesus," said Luke, his eyes wide.

Althea nodded and went on. "Laws were passed over the years to end slavery, some even by the Italian occupiers, but it took the Emperor to complete the job. So then my parents were free to marry. But, even so, there was nasty class prejudice against ex-slaves like my parents."

Abeba took Kofi's hand. Kofi was watching Luke closely.

"So when my mother got pregnant with me, they decided

they would rather have their child be a citizen of a country with more freedom and opportunity. So Mama and Papa took a leap and settled in Detroit."

Luke saw anger in Kofi's eyes. Luke slid the truth-shaker to him.

"Your turn sir."

Kofi gripped the shaker hard. "All right. White boy, you have nothing in common with my daughter and no understanding of her life."

"Papa!" Althea protested. Kofi held up a hand to silence her.

"As you have heard, my wife and I know something about hatred and bias. Class, religious, and racial hatred. The whole menu. Your marriage would attract the worst bigots, white and black, and bring her nothing but grief." He set the shaker down hard.

Luke stared at Kofi. Finally he said, "So what is your question, sir?" Kofi glared at him.

"I'm sorry sir. How about these? What can I bring to her life? Love and trust. How can I protect her? Any privilege my skin gives me, I will use for her. I have given this a lot of thought. Yes, I may be naive about life for a black woman in America but I've learned a lot from Althea. I'll be learning for the rest of my life."

He leaned toward Kofi and his voice became quiet but intense. "I will fight with all my heart to protect Althea and make her life as wonderful as I can." He pushed the shaker toward Althea. "We haven't heard much from you. Any questions?"

Althea rolled the shaker between her fingers while she thought.

"How did you fall in love with me?" she asked, smiling.

"Oh come on, I've told you many times why I love you," Luke protested.

"Not why, how. What was the process? I'm sure my parents would like to hear." Althea and her mother grinned while Kofi scowled.

"As you wish. I was sitting in Dominick's restaurant in Ann Arbor with Harry three years ago today. But you know that. You walked in."

"Go on," she said.

"I was struck with your beauty. Literally. Like a wonderful concussion, the only part of my brain that worked was filled with you." Kofi rolled his eyes. The two women looked at Luke with affection.

"That lasted about a minute…"

"What!" said Althea.

"Oh, I still was thinking how beautiful you were. But I recovered enough to talk with you. And so I fell even harder for you. I love your voice. Contralto, I guess they would call it if you could sing."

"Hey!" she protested. Abeba laughed.

"And since then, talking to me with that voice, I've learned how smart you are, which makes you even more
attractive, if that's possible. I've learned you have a strong heart, a loving heart. And that's about it. Oh wait, like me, you love science fiction. That makes it even more fun to be with you."

"Fun? Science fiction?" Kofi snorted, "Are you a child?"

Althea answered before Luke could respond. "No, he definitely is not."

Kofi had the grace to look awkward.

#

The conversation ranged over many topics. Althea's relatives in Ethiopia, Luke's work as a flight instructor, life with his uncle on the farm in Kansas, politics in Detroit. As he felt the dinner winding up, Luke touched the small box in his jacket pocket. *Should I? No, wait until we're alone.*

Althea held up her hands. Her parents and Luke turned to her.

"I have an announcement. When my residency ends next month.,,," The others raised their glasses in a silent toast.

".. I will go to work at a hospital in Nicaragua for six months."

Luke felt his stomach drop. He met Abeba's eyes.

She gave him a look of sympathy but said "Althea, that's wonderful."

Kofi said, "Why Althea? Aren't there plenty of patients in Detroit to care for?"

Or in Nevada, Luke thought.

"Papa, I've lived in Michigan my whole life and I want to see more of the world before I settle down. It's just six months."

Luke put on a smile and squeezed her hand. "That's great, darlin'."

#

Hours later, Althea met Luke at the hotel. She had a small overnight bag. They kissed standing in his doorway. He took her hand and led her into the room. Shutting the door, he asked, "So how did I do?"

Althea flopped into an armchair. Luke could see the fatigue on her face after a long shift at Providence Hospital and the long lunch with her parents. He sat on the ottoman, lifted her feet onto his lap, threw her shoes aside, and massaged her feet. She groaned in pleasure.

"You did great. Mama loves you and Papa finds you acceptable."

"And how about you?" he asked.

"Mmm, you'll do."

He stopped rubbing her feet. "Darlin'?"

"What?" She opened her eyes. He took something from his jacket pocket. Althea sat up to see it. The truth-shaker.

"Althea, what are you afraid of?"

"What do you mean?"

"When I told your father that I hope to marry you someday, he was about to light into me. But you had nothing to say about it. Am I crazy to hope for a life with you?"

"No! It's just…". She stopped.

"Are you afraid of what people will think? Like your father said?"

"No. I mean, maybe a little."

"If not that, then what?"

Althea's face scrunched up, almost in tears. Luke felt like a total jerk. He said, "Darlin', it's OK if you don't…"

"I've always been alone," she said quietly, "An only child. Super-protective parents. I was awkward and taller than the other kids, even most of the boys. Some called me 'The Stick' or, if they had met my parents, 'The African'. I was born here but my family wasn't like other families. I didn't share the same history in America as the other kids. So freakin' ironic! Other kids would mention that their parents fled from Jim Crow laws or that their great-great-grandparents were slaves. My parents were slaves! But I never told anyone because my parents still carried shame about it, especially Papa."

Luke moved closer and took her hand.

"My parents pushed me hard to excel in school, which made me even geekier to the other kids. So I took shelter in science fiction. Stories where it was cool to be different! And smart! I got used to being alone." She squeezed his hand.

"And now you're in my life. I don't quite know what to do with you. I want to open up and let you in but I'm afraid. I'm sorry. Maybe I can finally get my head straight if I skip town for a while." She smiled, just a little. "Is that an honest enough answer for you?" He nodded.

She asked, "Can you wait for me?"

He kissed her hand.

"As long as it takes."

Chapter 4: The Man in the High Castle

December 18, 1972

Smith pushed the drug-addled old billionaire in a wheelchair through the lobby of the Intercontinental Hotel in Managua, Nicaragua and into an elevator. When the doors opened on the top floor, they saw a mouse scurry past.

"Disgusting! I won't stay in this pigsty!" the old man yelled.

"Yes sir, Mr. Hughes! We'll move you immediately." Smith pushed the elevator button for the floor below, where the rest of Hughes' staff members were staying. One was walking by as the doors opened.

"Joe, stop." The man's eyes widened when he saw the billionaire. "We need to move Mr. Hughes to another hotel right now. No questions. Find one and book the entire top two floors. Move all our staff to the floor below Mr. Hughes. Call me on the limo phone when it's ready." Joe nodded dazedly.

Smith waited behind the wheel of the limo. He listened to Hughes fussing in the back seat, getting agitated as the drugs wore off. *Come on, come on*, thought Smith. Finally the car phone rang. Smith snatched up the receiver and listened.

"OK, got it. Directions?" he said, "Right." He hung up. *The Gran Hotel.*

December 23

Althea left the hospital after her shift and started walking back to her place, carrying a flashlight for safety's sake. It was after midnight but the air was still hot and humid, even though it was only two days before Christmas. Nicaragua was definitely not Michigan. Her visit would be over in a week and she'd return to the slushy streets of Detroit. She passed in front of the Gran Hotel and waved to the doorman. He had brought his daughter with her broken arm into the emergency room some weeks back.

"Hola Ernesto. Como esta tu hija?," Althea said in her pretty-good Spanish. Ernesto was kind enough to answer in English.

"I'm fine, Doctor. And Aura is back to playing football with her brothers. After meeting you, she wants to be a doctor, too."

Althea smiled and turned to go. The sidewalk moved like a giant serpent was passing beneath it. She fell and the pavement rose up to hit her. The high sound of shattering windows and the low rumble of collapsing walls filled the air. She got her feet under her and staggered to the middle of the street. The five story hotel had collapsed.

Earthquake, she thought.

Althea stared in horror at the pile of concrete, brick, and glass. Dozens of people must have been killed in a few seconds. She heard a faint cry from the top of the rubble, where the penthouse had been. She saw Ernesto nearby looking dazed. She called to him to follow her.

"Ernesto! Ven conmigo!"

She was surprised that she still gripped her flashlight. All lights in the city seemed to be out. The two of them picked their way to the rubble of the top floor, following the faint cries for help. A section of

roof lay at an angle and Althea saw a low opening beneath it. She crawled under the roof. An old man lay near a toppled heavy armchair. The chair was all that had kept him from being crushed. Althea was confused. His cries had been in English and he had been in the penthouse of the hotel so she assumed he was a wealthy tourist but he looked like a beggar, with long scraggly gray hair and a ragged beard.

"Are you hurt?" she asked.

"I don't know," he answered weakly.

"Can you move your legs?" A pause.

"Yes."

"Then crawl toward me. And hurry. There might be aftershocks coming."

She realized Ernesto was next to her when he reached to help pull out the man. The three of them slowly worked their way off the rubble and into the street. Althea was surprised but glad to see an old sedan pulling up to the curb. Two men got out.

"Por favor llevanos al hospital," she said.

The old man seemed unhurt but was probably in shock and she could help other victims best at the hospital. Then she saw the pistols the men carried. One gun barrel turned toward her. Time stopped. She felt like she was staring into a bottomless black pit.

"No dispare!" she heard Ernesto bark.

Amazingly, they lowered their guns.

"Ella es la doctora del viejo. Llevale con nosotros," Ernesto said.

I'm the old man's doctor? What is happening?, Althea wondered.

Ernesto held open the rear door of the sedan.

"Please Doctor, we must leave right now. We will take you to a safe place."

Althea wanted to say '*No! Take us to the hospital*!' but the guns frightened her. She got into the backseat of the car. Ernesto carefully sat the old man next to her before he also got in. The two gunmen sat in front. Althea thought of jumping from the car and running but she saw that the back seat door handles had been removed. The sedan moved off slowly as the driver navigated around the rubble in the
street. They seemed to be heading out of the city. Althea looked at the old man.

"Sir, I'm a doctor. How are you feeling?" He turned and looked at her with mild surprise.

Yeah, haven't met many black female doctors, have you?

"I think I'm OK, Doctor. Thank you."

He looked out the car window. "Where are we going?"

Althea said, "Yes Ernesto, where *are* we going?"

"Someplace safe" was all he would say.

They drove down country roads for what felt like an hour. She wondered if they were taking a convoluted route to keep her from being able to later guide the police to the 'safe place'. This helped calm her somewhat; if they were just going to kill her and the old man, they wouldn't have bothered.

They pulled up to a dark, low farmhouse. The two gunmen helped the old man into the house and left Ernesto to deal with Althea. She was tempted to run off into the darkness but didn't. The gunmen probably knew the area well and she'd likely just fall into a ravine. Kerosene lamps came on in the house.

"Please, Doctor, come inside and I will explain," Ernesto said.

She went in. The furnishings were cheap but clean. The main room was empty, so they must have put the old man into what looked to be the only bedroom.

"Ernesto, what...," she started to say.

The building shook and the earth rumbled. They staggered a bit but the aftershock was milder than the quake had been. She heard a cry of distress from the bedroom. Althea went in and saw the old man on a bed. One of the kidnappers pointed his pistol at her. She glared at him and he lowered the gun. Althea was exhausted and angry. She went to the bed and examined her fellow prisoner as best she could by the light of a lantern. He was scraped up a bit but appeared intact. She tucked a blanket over him and he seemed to doze off. Ernesto came in.

"All right, Ernesto, what is happening? Who is this?"

Ernesto waved the two gunmen from the room, gestured for her to sit on the other small bed, while he took the one chair.

"Doctor, I am sorry you have been caught up in this but we couldn't leave you for the police to question. Once I ordered my men not to shoot you, you would have been able to point the police toward me. Also, I realized that Señor Hughes might need a doctor's attention."

Her eyes widened. "Hughes? Howard Hughes?"

She remembered the newspaper report that the reclusive American billionaire was visiting Managua but it was hard to believe this gaunt, raggedy old man had a single centavo to his name, let alone billions.

"Are you sure you kidnapped the right man?"

Ernesto smiled.

"Yes Doctor. Though he was very private and shielded by his men, the maids had to see him now and then and they described him to me. Apparently his staff fed him a steady stream of drugs, which helps explain his sad appearance. My men were coming to steal him away tonight."

"So what now, Ernesto?"

"I'm afraid you will have to remain with us until we can arrange a ransom for Señor Hughes. Then you will be free to leave."

Really? she thought, but she didn't press the point for now.

"Doctor, I am sorry the accommodations here are so primitive; we will try to make your stay as comfortable as possible."

Christ, he sounds like I'm checking into the Gran Hotel.

Ernesto stood up. "Doctor, I will see you in the morning. I must find out if our families are safe after the earthquake. If you need anything...".

"I'll call Room Service."

Ernesto gave an uncertain smile. He left. She heard the lock on the door click. She glanced at Hughes on the other bed. He was snoring away. Exhausted, she dragged a blanket over herself. She was asleep in seconds.

Chapter 5: Rainbow's End

Harry Remains leaned back in the swivel chair in his tiny office, feet on his desk. His hair was shorter now and he wore tailored suits and fine Italian shoes instead of bell-bottom jeans and sneakers.

Am I The Man now?, he thought idly, *Oh well, it's 1972. The sixties are over.*

He enjoyed his work at The Lucky Leprechaun, his family's casino and hotel. He took a nerdy pleasure in monitoring all the financial and legal details of the business. First in his family to go to college, he expected to be Chairman of the Board someday. His dad and uncles were old school, coming from a long line of bookies, gamblers, and legally ambiguous characters. He, on the other hand, knew that the greatest wealth was to be made working with The System, not against it. So he was trying to clean up their act and make The Lucky Leprechaun an operation he could run with a clean conscience. For the moment though, on a quiet Christmas Eve morning, he was happy to just enjoy his coffee and the New York Times.

Harry opened the paper to the front page. '*Thousands Dead As Quakes Strike Nicaraguan City*'. His feet hit the floor as he sat up fast. *Althea!* He scanned the article quickly. Ten thousand or more dead. Most of the city in ruins. Fires burning out of control. He grabbed the phone and tried to call her home in Managua. No answer. He tried the hospital there. No answer. Same for the US Embassy. *Stupid!* He thought. The paper had said all utilities were knocked out. An image of Althea crushed under a building flashed through his mind. He closed his eyes and took a slow deep breath to calm himself. What to do? Harry set his frantic, animal-brain panic to one side and consulted with the rest of his mind, the parts that took in data, found patterns, and made plans. A memory flashed up, his Da giving him a wry smile and saying "Boyo, you don't always think best but, by God, you do think fast." And so he did. A plan emerged.

Harry called the Air National Guard Base in Indian Springs. Althea was probably fine and helping quake victims, he told himself. But Luke wouldn't sit and wait for news, not with

Althea in danger. Harry wouldn't put it past his impulsive friend to steal a National Guard plane, fly to Managua, and get arrested. The airbase telephone operator connected him.

"Lieutenant Priss."

Thank God. "Luke, it's Harry. You need to get here as fast as you can."

"Why? What's up?"

"First, just trust me and promise you'll get here ASAP."

"OK, fine, but why?"

"Major earthquake in Managua last night. Haven't been able to contact Althea."

Harry heard his sharp intake of breath.

"What's your plan, Harry? You must have one."

Yeah, we know each other, don't we? Harry thought.

"You get to Sky Harbor Airport, hanger seven. Bring your passport. Our casino has a plane there. I'll have it prepped. You fly us down to Managua. We find Althea. I'm sure she's fine…."

"Right," Luke said, "I should reach there in two hours. One small glitch: when my commander sees I'm gone on Monday, he'll declare me AWOL. That could hinder us if we need government support to find my girl."

"Give me the names of everyone in your chain of command. I'll find some kind of leverage. By the time you get here, I'll have things arranged."

Luke gave Harry some names and hung up. Harry called the airport to get the plane ready, then started calling other casinos.

"Sid? Harry Remains, from The Lucky Leprechaun. I've got a list of some officers from the Indian Springs airbase who want me to advance them some credit. Would you mind telling me if any of them owe you money? Great."

Eventually, Harry found what he needed. He called the airbase again and asked for the Commander. Luckily, he was at the base though it was Sunday.

"General Cosgrove? This is Harold Remains, manager of The Lucky Leprechaun in Los Vegas. I was just talking to Joey Mangione about various casino business issues and your debt to Joey came up."

"How is that your concern, Mr. Remains?" the General

asked coldly.

"I'll put it plainly, General. I need the services for a week or so of one of your men for a perfectly legal, in fact humanitarian, disaster relief mission. For your assistance as a consultant on this mission, I will buy and forgive your debt to Mr. Mangione. All done quite discreetly, of course. But I need Lieutenant Luke Priss put on special assignment right now." A long pause.

"Disaster relief, you say?"

Harry helped the General rationalize his decision for a few more minutes and finally got his agreement. Then Harry made other arrangements. A couple of hours later, he was standing outside the hangar when Luke pulled up in his red and white Thunderbird.

"Ready?" said Luke.

"Yep."

But Luke still took time to inspect the ten-seater business jet inside and out. Harry knew that Luke was itching to race to Althea but he appreciated Luke's methodical discipline. Luke could control his impulses when it mattered.

"We have a flight plan to Houston to refuel then on to Managua. About nine hours total," Harry said.

Luke didn't talk much during the flight. Harry felt like a chatterbox by comparison.

"So one of our casino's less-than-lucky customers offered this plane as collateral on a loan." Silence.

"I managed to contact the airport in Nicaragua; the runway is undamaged and cleared for planes to land. They're expecting us." Nothing. Harry gestured to boxes stacked in the back of the plane.

"We're loaded with medical supplies, water filters, and other emergency stuff. Althea's probably fine and busy at her hospital. When we show up, you know she's going to give us that eyeroll she does. But she'll be happy for the supplies and to see you for Christmas. I figured that while we're going to visit her, we should actually try to help out as best we can."

Luke said quietly, "Harry, what if she's dead?"

Long pause while Harry looked out at the bright blue sky.

"Well, we still help the injured down there because that's

what she would do. We do that to honor her. Then we bring her home."

Luke nodded. They flew on.

Chapter 6: Caves of Steel

"Hey Ugly, how's it hangin'?" the guard asked Ted.

Ted was in the cafeteria eating breakfast. No one called him Ted anymore. He had learned to answer to his prison nickname. After his attempt to bomb the Undergraduate Library at UM, the newspapers had labeled him 'the UGLi Bomber' and that was that. Ted sighed. He let humiliation feed his anger at The System. Rage kept him focused on his two dreams. One, escape from prison. Two, saving the planet from environmental destruction by destroying technological civilization and killing billions of people-parasites. Kill them all.

Putting on a smile, he looked up from an essay he was reading on using prime numbers to encrypt information. "Good morning Bob. How are you doing this beautiful day?"

"Yeah fine. Hey Ugly, get your ass down to the auto shop. My cousin needs you to fix something for him again and he's waiting for you there."

"Right away, Bob," Ted said as he picked up his meal tray.

Ted had made good use of his time in prison. He was a model prisoner so he was now a trustee, with more freedom of movement than most. His PhD was in mathematics and his brother would send him math journals which he enjoyed reading. But he also studied chemistry and electronics and he picked up the practical fields quickly. Three years into his twenty-year sentence, he felt he was ready for the next step.

Ted entered the auto shop. It was intended to give prisoners some training they might use to find work on the outside. And the prison staff and their friends got cheap repairs on their cars and trucks. Ted had convinced the prison administrators to set up a corner of the shop for working on electronics, like TV and radio repair. Ted saw the guard's cousin waiting by the worktable.

"Good morning, Mr. Corbin," Ted said, "What can I do for you?"

"Hey Ugly. You can fix my CB radio, that's what," Corbin said, "I'm headed up north on Thursday for a solo fishing vacation and the damn thing flaked out on me. I like playing it safe and don't want to be, uh ..."

"Incommunicado?"

Corbin stared at him blankly.

"Out of touch."

"Yeah, whatever. Think you can have it fixed by then?"

"Sure thing, Mr. Corbin. Come back on Thursday, say at noon? It will definitely be ready for you. Ready to go," Ted said with a smile.

Chapter 7: With Folded Hands

Sunlight coming through the wrought-iron grill over the window woke Althea from a fitful sleep. She heard a knock on the door then a key in the lock. Ernesto entered the room. "Hola, Doctor...," he began.

Groans came from the other bed. Hughes was tossing back and forth. Althea sat up, wide awake now. Whipping off her blanket, she went to Hughes and examined him, this time under the light of day. She was quick and thorough but gentle. When she exposed Hughes' arms and legs, she could see track marks.

"He's going through withdrawal. Do you know what he was taking?"

"No. And his supply is under the rubble of the hotel."

"Have you contacted his people yet? Maybe they can provide some while you negotiate with them?"

Ernesto slumped wearily. "Doctor, it has only been eight hours. And we have a slight problem with our plan; it seems that Mr. Hughes' entire staff was killed in the earthquake."

"Oh," she replied. Then "Ernesto, how is your family?" He smiled slightly.

"Doctor, you are kind to ask, given your current circumstances. My family is safe. My men were not so fortunate. They have each lost family members."

"Oh, I am so sorry to hear that. Please tell them that I will pray for their families."

Ernesto nodded. "That is very kind of you, Doctor. Now, what can we do for Mr. Hughes?"

"I need medical supplies. I'll make you a list. Can you provide some marijuana? Tourists must ask you that all the time, yes?"

Ernesto look sheepish. "I should be able to, yes."

"Good. Try to get a sativa strain, if possible. That should reduce his pain. Now Ernesto, I have a request."

"Yes, Doctor?"

"Release me. Mr. Hughes is very uncomfortable but not in immediate danger, I think. I can instruct you and your men in his care. There are many injured people at the hospital,

I'm sure, who could use my help more. The police have no reason to question me. I give you my word that I will not inform on you, if that helps, because, frankly, it's more important to me to help quake victims than it is to stop your fund-raising project." Ernesto gazed at her thoughtfully.

"One moment Doctor. I must discuss this with my men." He left, locking the door behind him. Althea could make out some of the conversation. One man suggested that, if they didn't need her to care for Hughes, why not kill her now? Her stomach sank. *Stupid! Why did I say that?* But Ernesto defended her, saying that if Hughes, the weak old man, took a turn for the worse, they would need her. The men agreed. Ernesto returned.

"I'm sorry Doctor. We can't release you for now. I will try to get you the supplies you requested."

Ernesto locked the door behind him. Althea sank to the bed.

Chapter 8: E for Effort

Harry sat in the passenger section of the plane, watching the scenery roll by. He looked up, startled, as Luke appeared in the aisle.

Luke said, "Don't worry, she's on autopilot. I need to use the can."

He gestured at the boxes of supplies stacked on the seats and floor behind Harry. Some were labeled 'Donado Por The Desert Inn' or 'Donated by The Sands Hotel'. A few other Vegas casinos were represented as well.

"What's with the labels?"

Harry said, "The paper said that Howard Hughes is visiting Managua. As a billionaire, he obviously would have a lot of influence there. So I called casinos he owns in Vegas and got permission to use their names on donated stuff."

"Why?"

"We're landing in a third world country under martial law. The government there has been known to force the people to donate blood which the government sells at a profit. They are literally bleeding their people dry. After the quake, corruption will be even greater. If I can pretend a connection to a billionaire, it will help us deal with the government. The Times said he has gone missing. If they find Hughes and bring us to him, well, I'll apologize for the pretense and hope he understands. Worst case, they toss us out on the street and we're no worse off. See the labels as protective spells."

Luke looked skeptical. "Speaking of protection...". He pulled a pistol from his duffel bag. "I brought one for you too."

Harry winced. "I wouldn't know how to use it."

"Suit yourself." Luke strapped on a holster.

"We'll play good cop/bad cop with the local authorities," he said, "I don't speak Spanish and you do. So you can negotiate while I loom ominously in the background."

Harry nodded and said, "Uh, the plane?"

"Yeah, yeah, give me a minute."

An hour later they were landing in Managua. The runway had no lights but the sun was just rising and there was enough daylight to land safely. Luke was opening the hatch and lowering the stairs as a truck pulled up and two soldiers climbed out. Harry walked up to confront them.

"Which of you is in charge?" he barked in Spanish. The smaller man stepped forward.

"I am Captain Añazco. Identi...".

Harry interrupted him curtly, "I am Harold Remains, representing Howard Hughes Corporation. Captain, we have little time. Please come aboard the aircraft." He gestured at the plane's steps.

The soldier moved up but stopped at Luke's large form blocking the doorway. Harry watched the silent power play. Luke stood there just long enough for Añazco to notice his holstered pistol and then meet his eyes. Having established that the plane was his territory Luke stepped aside before he would trigger a display of force by the Captain. Harry approved. *Not all negotiations are verbal*, he thought, as he followed the soldier onto the plane.

"Captain," Harry said, "We have come to deliver these medical supplies, generously donated by Señor Hughes' businesses, to your hospitals. We also require your help in finding Señor Hughes so we may determine his condition and assist him. Can you take us to him?"

Harry knew that he and Luke could have headed straight to the US embassy and asked for any word on Althea and they would try that soon. But then they would just be two more tourists out of hundreds churning through an overloaded system. Recruiting help from the dictator's stooges could be useful. So following his own rule of using The System, not fighting it, Harry played the Captain.

Añazco's eyes flicked over the boxes of supplies. Harry could see his calculation: Should he confiscate the supplies and sell them on the black market? Or help Harry and curry favor with General Somoza? Añazco leaned out the door and called commands to the other soldier. He turned back to Harry.

"Señor Remains, we will deliver you and these supplies to the hospital. I am sorry to report to you that Señor Hughes is missing. The Gran Hotel, where he was staying, was destroyed. This morning the rubble was searched but his body was not found.

I assure you that we are diligently trying to locate him."

Harry's eyes narrowed. *Good, then we can milk the Hughes scam a bit longer.*

Añazco looked relieved when Harry did not explode at him.

"Alright Captain, take us to the hospital. It seems our stay here will be longer than I thought. I expect you will provide us with help in our own search for Señor Hughes." A statement, not a question.

"Of course, Señor Remains, whatever we can do."

Luke spoke quietly in Harry's ear.

"We need to top off the plane's tanks now, before the fuel disappears from the airport."

Again, Harry appreciated Luke's thoroughness.

"Captain, Mr. Hughes will need this plane fueled immediately and ready for whatever service he requires."

Añazco almost saluted.

"Right away, Señor Remains."

Within the hour, they were driving past the General El Retiro Hospital where Althea worked as a visiting physician. Or had worked. Harry and Luke watched grimly as the truck passed the hospital. They didn't ask to stop but simply stared at the ruined building, with its sagging roof and cracked columns. The truck slowly maneuvered around rubble in the street.

Añazco said, "All four hospitals in the city were made unusable by the earthquake. We are taking you to the largest field hospital we have set up."

The truck pulled up to a city park covered in tents. The Captain found a medical worker who took them to the doctor in charge.

Harry introduced himself and said, "Doctor, my pilot and I have come from the United States with some supplies that we hope can help here. I'm sorry we couldn't carry more on our plane."

The exhausted doctor nodded and thanked them. Harry wanted to speak to him privately so he asked Luke to take Añazco and go unload the truck.

"Doctor, a friend of ours was working at the General El Retiro Hospital and we're trying to find her. Do you know Doctor Nespla?"

The doctor smiled.

"Yes. Althea. Very serious but very caring. The last time I saw her was the day of the earthquake. Yesterday?" the doctor said, shaking his head wearily. "I'll ask the others if they know anything."

"Thank you, Doctor." He saw the Captain returning from the truck.

"Oh yes, Doctor, might you also know anything about the American Howard Hughes? Very tall, thin gentleman?" The Doctor stared at him blankly.

"I have heard of him, yes, but I have no idea where he is. Shall I ask the others about him as well?"

"Yes, please." Harry turned toward the approaching soldier.

"Captain Añazco, my pilot and I will be sleeping aboard our plane later but for now we will be pursuing our own search for Mr. Hughes. Can you provide us with a vehicle and a way to contact you, our liaison to your government?"

The title pleased Añazco, as Harry knew it would.

"Yes, Señor Remains, I will return shortly with a car that you may use as you wish. If you need me, please just stop any soldier and direct him to contact me with your requirements."

He left in the truck. Harry turned to Luke, who was standing there looking grim.

"Luke, the Chief Doctor has not seen Althea since the quake. He'll ask around about her. Añazco will be loaning us a car soon. I'd say you and I should lend a hand here while we wait for word." Luke nodded silently.

Best to keep him busy, Harry thought.

For the next few hours, Luke and Harry did grunt work at the hospital to free up the staff. They moved the injured on stretchers, emptied bedpans, hauled water, and fueled lamps. Finally a woman, a nurse, approached Harry and Luke.

"Señores, I worked with Doctor Althea. Last night we talked for a moment in front of the hospital after our shift. We both left the hospital at the same time, after midnight. But we went in opposite directions so...," she finished with a sad shrug.

Harry translated for Luke and thanked the woman. A soldier showed up and dropped off a car for their use. The sun was going down.

"OK Luke, so we know Althea wasn't in the hospital when it went down, That's good news. But we can't really continue the search until morning. And we're both whacked. Let's go back to the plane."

Luke nodded. They slowly drove back to the airport. The plane looked untouched. Someone had put the equivalent of 'Keep Out. Government Property' signs on traffic cones set around the plane. Harry said, "I hope that's another protective spell and not theft by our liaison Añazco." They boarded the plane.

Luke said, "I'll use an air mattress on the floor. You take the bed in back. I'm going to check the fuel level." In a few minutes they had bedded down and doused the lights.

Harry said, "Tomorrow we check the US embassy for any help they can give. We'll find her soon, Luke."

"I'm staying until I do, Harry."

"We're both staying."

"Yeah. Thanks Harry."

Chapter 9: The Search

Harry woke up with the sun on his face. He was disoriented for a second then remembered where he was. He heard Luke moving about, got up and hit the can.

During a quick breakfast of Wheaties, they consulted a map of Managua they had found in the car. They drove to the house where Althea had been staying. Harry was relieved to see that it seemed intact. A knock on the door was answered by an old woman.

"Señora Gonzales?" Harry said.

She stared at them for a few seconds then said, "Luke! Harry!" with a big smile. This was odd since they had never met her. She waved them into the living room and sat them down.

"Althea talks about you two so much that I just knew who you were the minute I saw you!"

"Yes, thank you. But we have come to find Althea. Is she…" The woman's face fell.

"She did not come home that night. I thought she must be staying at the hospital to help, but then I found out the hospital was gone, destroyed." Her eyes teared up.

"She had told me that you two were smart and brave but a little crazy. Can you please find her?" she said anxiously.

Harry said, "Yes, Señora, we will." He stood up. Luke looked at him.

"Nothing?" Harry shook his head.

"Harry, can you ask if we can see Althea's room?" Harry did and the old lady gave Luke a sad smile. She showed them to Althea's small bedroom. Luke stood in the doorway, hesitating to enter. Harry remembered when Althea told Luke that she was leaving the country for a while, to volunteer at the hospital. Luke had told Harry sadly, "I guess she needs some space from me. So be it."

Now Harry watched Luke. He seemed blocked by a force field, not wanting to violate Althea's private space. Then Luke took a deep breath and stepped into the bedroom.

There wasn't much to see in the neat little room. No clues as to her whereabouts. Harry saw a framed photo on the nightstand of Luke and Althea that Harry had taken at the World Science Fiction Convention. Wearing costumes and looking goofy, grinning for the camera. Luke touched the picture but left it.

"Let's go Harry."

Harry asked Señora Gonzales to send word through the chief doctor if she heard anything. They drove to the US embassy and waited for an hour just to find that there was no word on Althea. She had not contacted the embassy after the quake and was not on any list of the dead or injured. Driving back to the field hospital, they found the nurse they had spoken to the night before.

Harry said, "Señora, this may be an odd question but do you recall the exact time you left the hospital that night?"

"No. I saw that it was after midnight and time for me to go but I spent a few more minutes talking to Dr. Althea in front of the hospital before we both left."

Harry translated the exchange for Luke. Luke reached into his back pocket and pulled out the map of Managua. He spread it out before them.

"Harry, ask her to point out the hospital, her home, and her usual route."

Harry had an idea of what Luke intended. He passed the request to the nurse and added, "Can you tell us where you were when the quake happened?"

"I was almost home, just in front of the bakery a few doors away."

"Did you stop along the way?"

She shook her head.

Luke said, "Harry, ask if she is willing to walk the route with us."

She was and, as her shift was done, she let them drive her to the site of the ruined hospital. They parked and got out.

Harry said, "Señora, please indulge us and walk home from here. We will follow you, Try to ignore us and just walk as you normally do. Please don't stop along the way."

She shrugged and started off. Harry glanced at his watch as he and Luke followed her. When they passed in front of the bakery, he checked his watch again. They arrived at her house and Harry thanked her for her trouble.

Harry said, "It took her fifteen minutes and forty seconds to walk to the bakery."

"And the quake hit after midnight, at 12:29:44pm," Luke said.

"Okay?"

"That means the nurse and Althea both left the hospital at 12:14:04." Harry gave him a sad look.

"Yeah, I know," Luke said, "it's stupid to be so precise but it's a start, OK?". They walked back to the ruined hospital.

Luke said, "According to the map, there's really only one route Althea would take to her place. You start walking there and I'll time you."

"No, you walk, I'll time. I've watched you two giants walking together and your pace is a better match to Althea's." They set off, Harry trailing Luke.

After fifteen minutes and forty seconds, Harry yelled, "Stop." Luke waited for Harry to catch up and they looked around. Harry pointed to an especially large pile of debris.

"We'll let that be the center of our search pattern." Luke checked the map.

"The Gran Hotel."

Chapter 10: Escape!

Corbin returned to the prison auto shop on Thursday. Ted gestured for him to pull his pickup into a bay of the garage and slid the big door down to block out the winter weather. Otherwise the place was empty, as the rest of the prisoners were at lunch.

"So is my CB radio ready?" Corbin said, as he climbed out of his truck. He was wearing his fishing outfit, with a big floppy hat covered in fishing lures.

Perfect, thought Ted.

"Yes, it's right here," he said, waving toward the bench.

As Corbin leaned over to look at the radio, Ted lifted a hand-made high-voltage stun gun and pressed it to Corbin's neck. The man arched convulsively and collapsed. Ted quickly stripped Corbin and traded clothes, slapping the floppy hat on his own head. Corbin's boots were too small for Ted so he put them back on Corbin and wore his own prison sneakers. No matter. He checked Corbin for a pulse. Dead. No matter. He propped the body on the chair at the workbench. Ted reached into a drawer and found the plastic bag of oxidizing pellets he had scavenged from the prison water treatment plant. He made sure the bag was well-sealed and stuffed it into the inlet of the 100-gallon gasoline tank sitting in the middle of the garage. Now he had to act quickly. He knew from testing that the gasoline would dissolve the plastic bag in about two minutes and release the oxidizer.

Ted drove the pickup past the guard at the gate, keeping his face obscured by the hat brim. The guard waved him out. Ted waved back. He was a block away when he heard the *whump* of the exploding gas tank. Ted felt great satisfaction as his plan unfolded so perfectly. It was like running through a mathematical proof and seeing the result reveal like a beautiful blossoming flower. But he wasn't done yet, had to stay focused.

He pulled into a Kmart parking lot and examined Corbin's wallet. $500 in cash, plenty enough for a nice two week fishing trip up north. Ted was heading north too but
just to Detroit for now. Ted went into the Kmart and bought toiletries, reading glasses, a tie, a jacket, and other clothes to make a decent white-collar costume, as well as a cheap suitcase. Then he

checked into a motel and had a nice long hot shower. Alone. *God, it feels so good to be alone.* He went to bed early. He had a lot to do in the next few days. As he lay there, he thought, as he had done so many times on his prison cot, that he had made his first bomb too soon. His plan had been sloppy and badly prepared. But since then he had trained himself and carefully worked out what he needed to do. Now he was ready. Deeply content, he drifted off.

Chapter 11: To Serve Man

Howard Hughes' condition improved rapidly. Ernesto never did bring any people injured in the quake for Althea to treat. She guessed he thought that was too risky. Althea and Hughes had long conversations; locked in the cabin, they didn't have much else to do. Althea learned that he had been in a bad plane crash years before that left him in a permanent state of pain. He had gradually gotten addicted to painkillers and his staff were more than happy to supply him with drugs while they 'managed' his financial empire.

"I'll tell you, Doc, I feel a lot better now. That wacky weed seems to help a lot. My head feels clearer. Calmer. Maybe that meditation you've got me doing has something to do with it too. Should I worry about becoming a zoned-out hippie?"

Althea smiled. "No, the strain of marijuana that Ernesto found for you has lower levels of the psychoactive factors and more of the cannabinoids that help with the pain."

And with appetite too, she thought with amusement. Their captors had been hard-pressed to supply enough food for the two of them. Hughes had been packing it in. Though he would always be tall and thin, he would soon lose his gaunt beachcomber appearance. Cutting his hair and nails had helped a lot. He had been rather embarrassed about that, saying that he had previously found being touched just too painful.

"Mr. Hughes...," Althea began.

"Doc, it really is OK to just call me Howard. You saved my life for Christ's sake."

"Alright, Howard, let's discuss this mess. Your strength and energy have improved a lot. Are you thinking of trying to escape? If you are then I would have to try too. If you were gone, our captors would just see me as an inconvenient witness to be eliminated. But I don't see how we...".

There was a rap on the door. Hughes seemed to change in an instant. He hunched over, his chin sagging, and his hands shaking. One of the guards came in with their dinner on a tray. He stared at Hughes as if he was a prize pig getting fattened for slaughter.

"Doctor, who is this? What's happening?" Hughes asked in

a pleading whine.

The guard shook his head, put the tray on the small table, and left. With the click of the lock, Hughes transformed, once again straight and alert.

"Thank you Howard," Althea said.

"No problem, Doc. We need to keep you employed, don't we?"

A nice way of saying 'alive', Althea thought.

Hughes said, "Anyway, Doc, I expect our best plan is to just wait. General Samoza was really happy when this billionaire came to visit Nicaragua. Though I guess he would have declared martial law after the quake and taken power once again, so maybe we should call him President Somoza? He was looking forward to me investing millions in hotels and casinos in Nicaragua."

"What does he have to do with this mess?"

"Don't you think he's noticed that I'm not in the rubble of the Gran Hotel? I'm sure he's got his men searching for me. I expect they will figure out that I've been kidnapped. And don't you think Ernesto, the doorman at the hotel, would be a prime suspect as a likely conspirator in such a plan? If they aren't questioning him right now, they will be soon. Once they torture and break him and find out where we are, they'll rescue us."

Horrified, Althea stared at him wide-eyed.

He shrugged. "Sorry, Doc. That just seems to me the way this will play out. I know you like Ernesto well enough and maybe he is protecting you a bit but remember, these are guys with guns who see a big payoff ahead. They'll kill both of us if they think they need to, to protect themselves and their families. So we wait."

She nodded slowly.

Chapter 12: The Demolished Man

Ted drove to the beautiful marble Main Library in Detroit. He went to the microfilm reading machines and searched through old copies of the Detroit Free Press and the Detroit News. Scrolling through obituaries from the early 1940s, he found one for a two year-old boy who had died in a car accident along with his family. Ted wrote down the details, left the Library, and visited the County Clerk office. He was wearing his suit and tie and reading glasses. As the clerk approached he put on his most winning smile.

"Hello, how are you today?" Ted said.

"Fine. How can I help you?" the older woman said.

"Well, I recently had a house fire and lost pretty much everything: tax records, important papers like my birth certificate, family photos, even my driver's license."

"Oh, that's terrible! Was anyone hurt?"

"No, thank goodness. Thanks for asking. We got out just in time but I couldn't even grab my wallet."

"Well, let's start putting that all back together, shall we? Except for the photos. What a tragedy!"

"Yes, thanks so much. My name is Frikes, Carl Frikes."

Ted left with a copy of a birth certificate, glad that death certificates were kept in a different file cabinet. Then he went to a Secretary of State office and applied for a driver's license, giving the clerk the address of the motel he was staying at.

"Yeah, I grew up in Vietnam. My parents were missionaries there. So I learned to drive but never had a driver's license there or in the US. Things were pretty Wild West there, if you know what I mean." The clerk was wide-eyed.

"Wow. You must have had quite some adventures."

"Not all good ones. My parents were killed by the Viet Cong and I decided it was time to come back home."

"Oh man, sorry to hear that."

"Thanks."

"You're going to need to take a driving test."

"Yeah, a friend brought me here in his pickup and loaned it to me for the test," Ted said, waving the truck key as proof. "He wandered off to get some lunch."

"Well, OK then."

In an hour or so, Ted walked out with a new license as Carl Frikes. As one more step in young Carl's resurrection, Ted drove to a Social Security office and gave a convincing argument as to why a 32 year old man didn't have a Social Security number. He provided his driver's license, birth certificate, and a letter of employment from the night clerk at the motel. The clerk had been happy to take $20 to let Ted type the letter on motel letterhead and had even signed it. Ted would have to wait a week or two to receive his new Social Security card by mail at the motel but he was willing to risk staying in the area that long. He even returned to the Library and got a library card, as well as a few books to read back at the motel.

As the last act in a long day, Ted drove west of Detroit to Eastern Michigan University. He went to the Library there and found Commencement programs from past years. He copied down the name of a graduate in the sciences and teaching programs. Then he went to the EMU Recorder's Office for another clerk scam.

"Hello, I'm Carl Frikes. I work at the University of Southern North Dakota in Hoople. I was asked by the administration there to check on a job applicant, since I'm in Michigan visiting family."

"How do you mean 'check on'?" asked the clerk.

"This guy," said Ted, pulling a note from his pocket and consulting it, "David Purdy. Apparently he said on his job application to our University that he graduated from EMU and got a teaching certificate too. But he didn't include copies. We just wanted to verify that it's all true."

"OK, let me see." Ted noted which file cabinets she went to. She laid two folders on the counter and opened them.

"Yes, it seems he graduated a few years ago and went on to get a teaching certificate. A copy of that is in the file too." She turned the forms for Ted to read.

"Can I ask you to make copies for me?" She hesitated.

"It could help one of your graduates get a job."

"Sure. Give me a minute."

Soon Ted left the building and strolled nearby, as workers left for the day. The lights went out in the Recorder's office. He waited another twenty minutes or so then returned to the office door. Locked. No matter. He had learned to pick locks from fellow inmates and had taken his set of hand-made tools with him from prison. He entered the office, flipped on the lights, and quickly found the cabinet holding blank forms and empty folders. He went to a typewriter at a desk and started copying the course data from David Purdy's records while entering Carl Frikes' fake personal info. His ego couldn't resist improving the grades a bit.

The door opened and a janitor stuck his head in.

"Hey, how you doing?" said Ted. He glanced at the nameplate on the desk. "I'm a friend of Betty's and she asked me to fix her typewriter. She didn't want to wait for the tech department."

"Whatever, man."

"I'll be out of your way in a few minutes."

Soon Ted created academic records for Carl Frikes and inserted them into the appropriate filing cabinet. The janitor didn't seem to wonder or care why Ted needed to open cabinets to fix a typewriter. Ted slid the drawer shut, feeling great satisfaction. He felt like a comic book superhero with a secret identity. He smiled. Time to return to the motel room, his Fortress of Solitude.

#

Ted took a long hot shower and lay on the bed. The next step in his plan would be to create an encryption system to send bomb threats to the FBI and the newspapers. He would write and send his Manifesto too. A good terror
campaign needed to get the public thinking and his long essay explaining how the human race and technology were destroying the planet would surely give them something to think about.

But for now, he was exhausted and would let himself do nothing important for a day or so, just as a treat. He twisted the knob on the TV, flipping through all eight channels. Nothing worth watching. He turned it off and picked up a copy of a science fiction novel, *Stand on Zanzibar* by John Brunner, that he had borrowed from the Library.

Ha, he thought, *Carl Frikes even has a library card. Carl, Carl, Carl. Must get used to that name. Can't be reacting if I happen to hear someone say 'Hey Ted!'*.

He started reading. The novel described an over-populated Earth in the year 2010. The world population had almost doubled, reaching a staggering seven billion. Society was falling apart.

Yeah. Falling apart. That's good. The only answer. He was fading. He roused himself a few times and read a bit more. When he reached the part in the story about an African country with a President named Obomi, he fell into a deep sleep.

Chapter 13: The Restaurant at the End of the Universe

As Luke walked past the Gran Hotel site, he watched a work crew removing the last bit of rubble. The streets had been cleared of debris and people were going about their business. Luke hadn't seen any looting or bodies for days. *Everyone wants to get back to normal*, he thought. He felt a spasm of panic and suppressed it. Every day, the world seemed to move further from Althea. Like the ground had opened up and swallowed her and everyone was happy to smooth it over and carry on.

Captain Añazco had kept Harry and Luke informed on the search for Howard Hughes. The bodies of hotel staff and guests killed in the earthquake had been removed and identified. The government had acted quickly, the morning after the quake, to verify that the billionaire was not in the top layer of rubble that had once been the luxury penthouse. Now after three weeks it verified via local newspapers that Hughes was not among the five thousand men, women, and children killed by the quake. Luke didn't give a damn about Hughes.

"Por favor," Luke said to an old lady carrying a basket of bread. Harry had taught him a few phrases in Spanish. By now their search had taken them blocks from the Gran Hotel rubble and still no results. He pulled a small photo of Althea carefully from his wallet and showed it to the old woman. She shook her head. Seeing the sadness in Luke's eyes she looked sympathetic and added "Buena suerte para ti". Luke had heard the wish for good luck a hundred times. It wasn't helping.

"Gracias, Señora." He checked his watch and headed back to the field hospital.

#

Harry saw Luke park and waved to him. He turned back to the Chief Doctor.

"Señor Remains, I have conferred with doctors at the other field hospitals. None have seen Althea, either as a doctor or patient."

As Luke walked up, the doctor added softly, "I have also

talked to those running the collection and processing of the dead. None have seen a body matching Doctor Nespla's description." Harry tried to put a positive spin on that as he translated for Luke.

"That's good news, Luke. Clean-up after the quake is almost done. So she must be out there somewhere."

"Then why hasn't she returned to her place or contacted the embassy?"

Harry could see that Luke was feeling hopeless. With little Spanish, he wasn't much help in questioning people. He put most of his energy into working at the field hospital. Harry was starting to wonder if Luke had decided Althea was dead. He couldn't bring himself to ask.

"Luke, let's go eat something. Doctor, we'll be back in an hour or so."

As they got into the car, Harry saw a note on the dashboard. He read aloud "El Pollo Psicodélico" and an address.

"The Psychedelic Chicken. I've heard it's a decent restaurant. Seems like someone thinks we should go there." He met Luke's eyes and saw his desperate need for a lead to Althea, any kind of lead.

"Give me a second," Harry said. He stepped out and waved down a passing soldier. They talked for a minute. Harry got back in the car.

"What, were you getting directions? We have a map," Luke said impatiently. Harry shrugged and waved for Luke to start the car.

They parked in front of El Pollo Psicodélico. The low building was seemingly undamaged by the earthquake. It was hard to miss, painted in fluorescent colors that imitated Peter Max artwork. The waiter led Luke and Harry to an empty table near the kitchen. They ordered lunch and ate silently. Luke wolfed his meal down while Harry ate slowly and methodically, twice asking the waiter to refill his water glass. Staring at Harry, Luke drummed his fingers on the table impatiently.

When Harry finally finished, wiping his mouth with the worn linen napkin, Luke said, "Well, the chicken was good but I was expecting something more somehow."

The waiter appeared and said, "Gentlemen, may I ask you

to follow me please?"

He led them through the kitchen and out the back door. The alley was empty except for an old sedan with the trunk open. The waiter pulled a pistol from under his white apron and pointed it at Luke.

He said politely, "Please remove your gun belt, place it on the ground, and climb into the trunk. Señor Remains, I would ask you to join him. Quickly please."

Luke slowly unbuckled his gun belt and set it down. The trunk lid lowered over Luke and Harry.

"Looks like we're being kidnapped," Harry said.

"Ya think?"

"I'm hoping it's by the same people that took Althea."

"What!"

"Yes, I've thought for some time that she was kidnapped. They probably took Howard Hughes as well. She was passing the Gran Hotel, where he was staying, when the quake hit. It's just too coincidental that they both went missing at the same time and place."

"Why the hell didn't you tell me this?"

"I wasn't sure. I'm still not. Maybe we've been taken because we're rich gringos. I've been talking to so many people about Hughes, using us as bait, that I'm hopeful the 'right' gang has taken us. But I need you onboard in case they're taking us to her. So here's my plan…".

"You have a plan for this? Unbelievable," Luke said angrily.

"Yes, I do. It's a little rough on the details and we'll have to be ready to improvise. But here's the basic idea…." They spent the next hour bouncing over bad roads in pitch darkness.

Chapter 14: The Changeling

On New Year's Day, Ted drove the pickup truck up north in Michigan and found a deserted, frozen lake. He walked out on the ice and saw that it was thin towards the middle. Putting the truck in first gear, he jumped out and let it roll out onto the lake. As he hoped, the truck broke through the ice and disappeared. If it was ever found the cops would trace it back to Corbin. They'd conclude that he had driven drunkenly onto the lake and drowned after exiting the truck. Ted walked back to the main road and hitchhiked south.

Three days later Ted, now Carl Frikes, sat in a high school office in Butte, Montana, after a long Greyhound bus ride. The Principal reached across the desk to shake his hand.

"Carl, it was a pleasure interviewing you. After all our phone calls, it's good to finally meet you in person. I can tell you right now you've got the job."

Ted smiled. "Thank you, sir. I look forward to meeting my students."

"Well, we're lucky to have you. Our math and science teacher recently informed us that she's pregnant so of course we'll have to let her go. Very fortunate that you were available. But I couldn't help noticing your suitcase in the waiting room. Don't you have a place to stay in town?"

"Well sir, I just got off the bus this morning and I'm embarrassed to say that getting to Butte used up most of my available funds. I was hoping to find a YMCA or such to stay at for the short term."

The Principal waved a dismissive hand. "Nonsense. You can bunk in my basement until you find a place of your own. I'll see what I can do to get you an advance on your pay."

"Thank you sir, you're very generous."

As soon as he could, Ted rented a small isolated house outside of town and bicycled to school every day. Even though the town had a population of only thirty thousand or so, it felt crowded to Ted. The house gave him a place to work in peace, in an area of beautiful foothills. Biking past the town's huge open pit copper mine, foul with toxic mine wastes, only energized him in his crusade. He would do his small part to destroy the warped technology killing the planet by striking at those leading that technology. The chemistry lab at the high school was useful for the after-hours production of homemade C4 explosive. Ted built a dozen elegant bombs. An ingredient was added to the commercial version of C4 that could be detected by security forces using sniffer devices. Ted did not include it. He couldn't risk mailing the bombs from the small post office in Butte, where everyone knew him. So he borrowed a car and made the five hour drive to Spokane. *A hassle but worth it*, he thought. He mailed his first bomb as well as three binders, one to the New York Times and two to the FBI. As he drove away, he felt the same satisfaction he had when escaping prison. *This is going to be fun.*

Chapter 15: Something Wicked This Way Comes

The trunk lid popped open and they were blinded by bright sunshine.

"Please gentlemen, try to exit quickly."

Luke clambered out. Harry slowly and clumsily followed him. A man stood to one side pointing a gun at them. Harry noted that the waiter had removed his apron. He waved them all into a small house. Yet another armed man stood in the otherwise empty living room. The waiter gestured to a large oak table.

"Please be seated," he said, just as he had in the Psychedelic Chicken.

Harry sat down but Luke remained standing while the waiter, *no, the ringleader*, thought Harry, entered another room for a moment. Althea came out. Harry expected Luke to rush to her but he didn't. Luke closed his eyes and let out a deep breath, as if he had been holding it for weeks. He opened his eyes and held out his hand. Althea took it and stood quietly close to him. No kiss, no hug, no passionate words. To Harry, the two looked like they were home together at last. And not captives at gunpoint.

"Ernesto, who the hell are these guys?"

A tall old man was standing in the bedroom doorway, wearing sandals and an ill-fitting white linen suit. Harry recognized him as the missing billionaire.

Ernesto said, "They have been nosing around, Señor Hughes. Occasionally asking about you but mostly about the Doctor. Let's all sit down and talk, shall we?"

Hughes walked feebly to a chair, Althea moving to take his elbow. The four of them sat along one side of the long table and Ernesto on the other. The two armed guards stood where they could cover them all, though they seemed most wary of Luke. Althea and Luke, holding hands, were relaxed and seemed oblivious to the danger they were in. Harry wished he could be as blissful. Maybe Althea was providing carc to Hughes and so had some value to the kidnappers but once they realized Luke and Harry did not they would, if they were rational criminals, dispose of them. Harry's mind raced to find a reason for them not to. Ernesto turned to Harry.

"I was hoping you could help us but you do not really work for Señor Hughes, do you?,"

"Well, I do help run The Lucky Leprechaun casino in Las Vegas but, no, that is not one of Mr. Hughes' properties. I just thought claiming to work for Mr. Hughes would be a useful fiction to get help from your government."

Hughes smiled. "Clever." Ernesto looked exasperated.

"Señor Hughes claims that none of his employees left in the United States has access to his bank accounts. He suggested we take him to a local bank and he would authorize a wire transfer. But his face is well-known to the public and the police would be called immediately so….no."

Harry said, "What ransom are you demanding?"

"One million dollars."

Harry looked at Hughes.

"I accept."

"Well, that was easy," said Harry.

"But Ernesto, I want to be released immediately," said Hughes, "I'll send the money to you after I'm safely out of your charming country".

"Please Señor Hughes, I am not an experienced criminal but I am also not an idiot."

"Look Ernesto, you know that General Somoza must be looking for me. Every day you keep me is a risk you don't want."

"Which is why my friends and I and our families have been, how do you Yankees say it, 'laying low'. And what assurances could you possibly give me if I release you? We would have no leverage."

Ernesto's eyes flicked over Althea. Harry realized that Ernesto was wondering if the bond between her and Hughes was strong enough to use her for that leverage.

"Our plane," Harry said.

All eyes turned to him.

"Excuse me?" Ernesto said.

"You can have the plane Luke and I flew in on. It's a Lockheed Jetstar and belongs to my casino. I'll sign it over to you if you release all four of us. I can write up an agreement here and now and we can wrap this up quickly."

Hughes nodded thoughtfully, "That's a nice plane. Worth about $2.8 million new."

Ernesto said, "And what would I do with a jet plane? I have set up a bank account in the Cayman Islands and that is where I need $1 million deposited."

Silence fell over the group.

Harry was surprised when it was finally Luke who spoke.

"Ernesto, do you trust Althea? I remember she wrote to me about helping your daughter."

Ernesto looked puzzled.

"Yes but…"

Luke continued, "And Althea, do you trust Harry to keep his word?"

"Always."

Harry felt a rush of pride.

"And do we all trust Mister Hughes, billionaire and master deal maker, to always follow his own financial best interests?" Ernesto, Althea, and Harry all nodded while Hughes scowled.

"Then I propose that Mr. Hughes buy the Jetstar from Harry for $1.4 million, half its fair market value, and that Harry then promise to pay Ernesto $1 million for housing and protecting Althea and Mr. Hughes during this time of disaster." Harry was impressed. Hughes looked skeptical.

Harry added, "Otherwise, Althea, Luke, and I could give Ernesto vows of secrecy and we fly away, leaving Ernesto to send bits of Mr. Hughes to his casino managers in Las Vegas to encourage them to pay the ransom. If lightly tortured, I can provide Ernesto with their names and phone numbers."

"OK, fine, I agree," said Hughes. Ernesto moved to the other end of the room and conferred quietly with the two guards for a minute. Finally, the three men turned to face the hostages. Ernesto had the grace to look apologetic.

"I am so sorry. We cannot accept those terms. Señor Hughes, please step away from the table."

The guards drew their guns.

Chapter 16: Watchmen

Hughes did not move. Ernesto shrugged. The guards pointed their pistols at Luke and Harry. Ernesto put his hands over his ears. Harry had a moment to think, *Killing us too loud for you?* The floor shook as something large stopped outside. The guards turned toward the door as it burst open.

"No se mueven!" shouted Captain Añazco as soldiers swarmed into the house. The kidnappers opened fire. Luke grabbed the edge of the heavy oak table and flipped it on its side. He yanked Althea behind it. Harry and Howard dove for cover as well. Bullets struck the table.

Harry yelled, "Captain, four hostages here! Stop shooting!"

"No disparen!" Añazco shouted. The gunfire stopped. Harry's ears were still ringing from the barrage of shots as he peered around the end of the table. The kidnappers lay in a widening pool of shared blood. Añazco ordered his men, all amazingly unharmed but still dangerously high on adrenaline and trigger-happy, to leave the house. Althea was the first hostage to emerge. She retrieved a first-aid kit from the bedroom and checked the kidnappers.

The guards were dead and Ernesto lay moaning in pain, shot in the shoulder. Althea bandaged his wound and told Añazco, "He needs to get to a hospital."

Captain Añazco glanced at Howard, who nodded.

"Immediately, Doctor. I will then deliver you all to the Presidential residence. President Somoza will…"

"No, Captain," said Hughes, "You will then drive us to our airplane. It's time for me to leave. I will communicate with President Somoza soon."

Añazco hesitated.

"And I will at that time, of course, express my deep gratitude for your daring rescue."

Añazco nodded.

Harry said, "About that rescue, Captain… what took you so long?"

"Señor Remains, when the soldier reached me with your message about a possible trap, we deployed as quickly as possible, but you had already left the restaurant. Fortunately, the cook there was finally willing to direct us to the kidnappers hideout."

Poor cook, thought Harry.

#

Althea sat in the back of the army truck with her eyes downcast and her expression pensive.

"You're thinking of staying, aren't you?" Luke asked.

Miserable, she said, "I don't know. I'm sure they could still use my help at the field hospitals. And you have to get back to your base, right? But I don't think I can bear being apart anymore."

Luke said, "So marry me."

"What? How does that…?"

In the darkened back of a truck, bouncing over potholes, with an audience of sweaty soldiers, a bloodied kidnapper, a billionaire, and a dear friend, Luke got down on one knee. Harry and Howard held his shoulders to steady him against the lurching of the truck. He pulled a small box from a pocket and opened it. Under moonlight, he showed her the ring inside.

Taking her hand, Luke said, "Marry me. We'll figure all the rest out. Together."

She smiled through tears. "You are crazy. OK. I mean, yes, I will marry you."

The men cheered.

"But I'm keeping my last name."

Chapter 17: Rite of Passage

They delivered Ernesto to the field hospital. Althea was greeted with hugs by the nurses while Harry explained to the chief doctor what had happened.

Althea said, "Doctor, I'm sorry I wasn't here to help after the earthquake. Can I...?"

He held up a hand. "No, Doctor Nespla. You have already helped so much during your time at the El Retiro hospital." He gestured at the tents around them.

"Believe it or not, our situation is settling down. We have much fewer patients now and we will be moving to a building soon. We greatly appreciate what you have done but I expect your hometown of Detroit can also make good use of your skills." He smiled at Luke and back at Althea. "Time to go home, I think?"

#

After inspecting the plane, Luke called the control tower to tell them he was setting course for Houston. Hughes interrupted him.

"No, let's go to Grand Bahama island. I own the Xanadu Princess Hotel there and if I go back to the States I'll have to deal with the damn IRS. So, no."

Luke shrugged and gave a new flight plan to the control tower. Hughes sat in the co-pilot's seat. Luke knew he had not been in the cockpit of a plane for years. Hughes seemed to enjoy the takeoff but once they reached altitude and leveled off, he unbuckled and stood up.

"Thanks for that. I'll go get Doc."

He left the cockpit. Soon Althea came in, leaned over, and kissed Luke long and slow. She held his face in her hands and gazed into his eyes.

"I've missed you, flyboy. But, to be honest, I am really tired after this adventure so I'm going to rest in back. You could join me but, you know, the plane. I'll see you later."

Patting his cheek, she left the cabin. Hughes returned.

"All good?"

Luke nodded. Hughes took the co-pilot's seat again.

"This is like a six hour flight, right? If you want to take a break at some point…?"

Luke looked at the old man. Hughes was, what, maybe sixty-seven? He had not piloted a plane for at least twenty years and wasn't in the best of health. Luke put it on auto-pilot and got up.

Waving at the controls, Luke said, "Just try not to kill us."

Hughes smiled and moved to the pilot's seat. Luke went back to be with Althea. As he passed, Harry looked up at him, startled.

"Tell me we're on auto-pilot."

"I think he'll be OK. Remember, this is a man who set a speed record flying around the world."

"Fine. But I think I'll go keep him company. I'll scream if we need you."

#

Harry sat next to Hughes, saying nothing.

After a few minutes, Hughes said, "So, The Lucky Leprechaun casino, eh?"

"Yep. It's small but I have high hopes for it."

"You the owner?"

"No, my Dad and uncles own it. I'm lawyer and financial officer."

"Offering to sell a 2.8 million dollar airplane to net only four hundred thousand doesn't seem like the smartest financial move."

Harry shrugged.

"It seemed like the wisest move at the time. But with Ernesto in custody, the deal is off. Sorry."

"Would you really have sent a million to Ernesto?".

"Of course."

"Why?"

Harry turned to look at Hughes.

"Because I said I would. I may be a lawyer but I keep my word. If not for his two thug friends, Ernesto might have accepted the deal. Instead, they were going to shoot Luke and me and maybe keep Althea for leverage, trusting that you felt some loyalty to her."

Harry didn't ask if Hughes actually did.

"Ernesto told me that my casinos in Vegas had flown in some medical supplies to Managua. Was that your doing?"

"Yes, I know the managers and got their OK to use the casinos' names. I hope they'll reimburse me when I get back. Hey, can you make a few calls when we land?"

Hughes said nothing for a minute. Harry wondered if he had been a bit too impertinent.

Finally Hughes said, "Doc talked about you and Luke often. And science fiction. A lot of science fiction."

"Yeah, SF is a common interest for the three of us. But, strangely, Luke is even more interested in Althea. He made it clear to her a few years ago that he wanted a life with her but he didn't even propose. Didn't want to pressure her, I suppose. I think Althea went to Managua to help at the hospital, of course, but also to get some head space to decide about him. Guess she has."

They sat quietly for a bit, just looking out at the blue sky.

Harry said, "You know, you and Althea don't have your passports. You're going to have to contact the US Consulate when we land."

"Can I ask you to take care of that? I just want to get to the hotel and not deal with all that nonsense."

"Sure. Shall I represent you generally while I'm on the island?"

Hughes nodded.

"More than that, if you're willing. For some reason, my entire upper level staff was in Managua for a pow-wow, probably because they thought the old man was about to kick off and they wanted to dicker over the spoils. Well, they're all dead now and I need to re-organize. Do you want to oversee my Vegas casinos and serve as my lead lawyer in general?"

Harry stared at him and finally said, "*I* know I could do that. But you don't really know me. What makes *you* think I could handle that?"

"Oh, as I said, Doc talked about you and Luke quite a bit

while we were locked up. When we weren't doing those damned yoga exercises of hers. I knew about The Lucky Leprechaun back from when I was buying up casinos. It was, frankly, a real dump. I didn't bother with it."

Harry wasn't offended. He had to agree with Hughes' assessment.

"But Doc told me how you turned it around. Pretty impressive, given the competition from my casinos."

"Thanks. And I would want to keep my hand in there, even if I'm working for you, for the sake of my family. But, again, why choose me?"

Hughes smiled. "Remember when Luke asked Ernesto about trust? Well, I trust Doc with my life and she trusts you. Good enough."

Harry stood up.

"OK, deal. I'm going to go make a list of a few hundred questions to ask you after you're settled in at the hotel." He left the cockpit. In a while, Luke returned and moved to sit in the co-pilot's seat but Hughes held up a hand.

"No, you can take over. I've had enough fun for now and you should probably handle the landing anyway."

As they switched seats Luke handed Hughes something wrapped in foil.

"Althea thought you might like a brownie. She says she has more she made at the house."

"Yeah, I was starting to feel a little edgy. Thanks."

They sat in companionable silence while Hughes munched his herbal snack. He licked the last crumbs from his fingers.

"So while we were involuntary roommates, Doc mentioned that you hope to become an astronaut."

"Yes, sometime after I get out of the Air National Guard, if there are any spaceships to pilot then."

"Doc also said you had some ideas about spaceship design that were a little unconventional. But she was fuzzy on the details. Tell me about those."

Luke knew he had to tread carefully. Hughes Aircraft had built the first American probes to land on the Moon and a host of missiles for the military. Hughes had been a decent practical engineer in his day and Luke did not want to look like an idiot.

"Before I get into the technical side, can I talk about the financial reasons behind my idea?" Hughes nodded.

"Right now the cheapest way to space is on the Saturn 1B rocket. But that still costs at least $4,000 to send a pound of anything into Low Earth Orbit. This keeps the market for space travel limited to a few communications satellites or to manned missions where the funding comes from a fickle government."

"So what's the alternative?"

"Do for spaceships what Henry Ford did for the automobile. Drop the price radically."

"And what do you think would happen then?"

"Hotels in orbit? Mining asteroids for platinum? Retirement homes on the Moon? Certainly servicing satellites. Space offers tons of resources and energy. Building the ships for that market could mean billions in potential profit."

"Christ, that sounds like a marketing pitch Harry might make," Hughes said wryly.

Luke flushed.

"Yeah, well, he and I have had long talks about this idea. Guess I picked up some of his financial enthusiasm."

"OK, enough about money for now, how would you carry out this grand vision?"

"Reusability, operations cost, and turn-around. Build a ship to fly thousands of times, like an airplane, not just once like the Saturn 1B. A ship that stays in one piece, not dropping expensive parts into the ocean. Use propellants that could be made available at any large airport. Design for re-launch in hours, not months. Fly, fly, and fly some more, to spread out the cost of the ship."

"But, really, is there a market for so many flights?" Hughes said skeptically.

"Not for huge ships the size of a Saturn or even a Delta. This would be a small ship that would carry only a few people or one or two tons of cargo to Low Earth Orbit. You could also fly VIPs or precious cargos on sub-orbital flights to anywhere on Earth in an hour. Wouldn't the military love to be able to pop up to orbit to observe a battlefield? The market for a small, cheap spaceship is much bigger than the market for huge rockets."

"But rockets aren't cheap to build. How would you reduce that cost?"

"I wouldn't worry too much about that at first. It might cost ten times as much to design and build as this jet did. But the cost to build is not the problem. It's throwing an expensive vehicle away after one flight that's dumb. Fly the ship a couple hundred times and you've paid for it in the first year."

"You said 'stays in one piece'. I saw proposals once by a Douglas engineer for single-stage rockets. Is that what you're talking about?"

"Not exactly. I think you mean Phil Bono. His ideas are interesting, mostly because he would reuse the rocket, not because it's single-stage."

"So what are you suggesting exactly? Time for details," said Hughes, a little impatiently.

"A winged ship that takes off like a plane. No jet engines but seven or eight rocket engines, maybe a version of the Pratt & Whitney RL10 engine. It takes off from an ordinary runway burning kerosene and liquid oxygen. The kerosene tank is full but the oxygen tank is almost empty, to reduce weight so the wings and landing gear can be smaller and lighter. Every pound we can shave from the ship means more cargo we can carry. It has only enough oxygen to get it up to 40,000 feet for a few minutes. There it meets a tanker plane, probably a KC-135, that hooks up with it and tops off the liquid oxygen tank. Then the ship unhooks, throttles up its engines, and pops up to orbit."

"So in-flight refueling, eh?"

"Yep. The military does it dozens of times a day, not a big deal. I've done it a few times."

"But in this case, you'd be pumping liquid oxygen, not fuel?"

"Right. The tanks on the KC-135 would have to be modified but that's easy enough."

"So this is really sort of a two-stage rocket system, with the KC-135 acting like a second stage."

Luke shrugged.

"Call it what you will. Maybe a Bono-style cone-shaped single stage would eventually be better for launching larger payloads. But this system would be cheaper to develop and operate."

They talked about the idea for the rest of the flight. Luke realized that he and Hughes, though they were a generation and billions of dollars apart, were both engineers hungry for a chance to just geek out with a peer and kick an idea around for the sheer pleasure of it. He expected that, when they landed, Hughes would go back to running his empire, Luke would focus on making a living and a life with Althea, and his ideas would be filed forever in his own mind under 'Wouldn't It Be Great If'. Luke answered what questions he could and was honest about the things that needed more study. He sensed when it was time to shut up and just let Hughes be.

Finally Hughes said, "You know, I set a world air speed record once, God, almost forty years ago. Lockheed holds the current speed record of Mach 3.1. How fast would your ship go?"

"Mach 27.5."

Hughes whistled.

"Sweet baby Jesus, let's build it."

Chapter 18: Foundation

It was late when they landed on Grand Bahama Island. Hughes holed up in the plane while Harry walked to the control tower and called the Xanadu Princess Hotel in Hughes' name.

"Yes, Mr. Hughes will require the entire top two floors of the hotel. Any guests that are moved will not be billed for their stays. Have the rooms prepared within the hour. When that's done send two cars to the airport to transport us. I'll meet them at the control tower. Understood? Thank you." He hung up.

Man, it's good to be King.

When the cars arrived, Harry sent the drivers back in one of the cars and drove their group to the hotel himself in the other. Despite being mellowed out on pot, Hughes still had some foibles, like minimal human contact. When they got to the Xanadu Princess hotel, Hughes stayed in the car while the others shooed away hotel employees and bundled Hughes into an elevator to the penthouse. They chose suites for all of them on the top floor and left the floor below empty, to be used later for meetings and business visitors. Hughes retreated to his suite. He was in bed when there was a knock on his door.

"Howard? May I come in?"

"Sure, Doc." Althea came in, carrying a pitcher and a tumbler of water.

Howard said, "Excuse me if I don't get up, Doc. I'm pretty bushed."

Althea put the water on his nightstand.

"It's distilled, just like you like it. You need to stay hydrated."

"Thanks Doc."

She turned to leave.

"Hey Doc."

"Yes?"

"Your folks came over from Ethiopia, didn't they?"

"Yes, back in '44, during the war. Mom was pregnant and wanted me born in the US."

"Ethiopia used to be called Abyssinia, right?"

"Yes, a couple of thousand years ago." Howard closed his

eyes.

"Goodnight Howard. Sleep well."

"Goodnight Doc."

Althea turned off the light and left, gently closing the door.

Howard lay in bed, in the hotel he had bought just the year before, thinking of a poem he had learned as a boy. Strange that it came back to him now.

In Xanadu did Kubla Khan a stately pleasure-dome decree.

He started to doze off.

It was an Abyssinian maid.
And on her dulcimer she played,
Singing of Mount Abora.
Could I revive within me
Her symphony and song,
To such a deep delight 'twould win me.

He fell into a sound, peaceful sleep.

#

In the living room of Hughes' suite, Harry told Althea and Luke, "I'm going to be up late dealing with the US Consulate, Customs, the hotel manager, and the Immigration Service. Hopefully, I'll see you all for breakfast. Goodnight." He left for his suite and they went to theirs.

Althea said, "Honey, I'm going to call and let my folks know I'm OK."

It was a long call. Althea's parents wanted to hear the whole story. Luke went off to shower and shave. Althea had to plead exhaustion to end the call. When they got to bed at last, Luke took her hand.

"Darlin', I want to apologize for spending most of the flight jawing with Mr. Hughes instead of being with you."

She smiled. "That's OK flyboy. I've learned what engineers are like. You both needed to release your pent-up geekiness."

She kissed him. "But now you're all mine."

Eventually they fell asleep in each other's arms.

Chapter 19: The Door Into Summer

The four met over breakfast in Harry's suite.

Hughes said, "We have a lot of important business to discuss. The top priority is the wedding." The other three stared at him blankly.

"For some reason, maybe because she was in shock after that shootout, Doc agreed to marry this lug," waving a hand at Luke.

Harry and Luke smiled while Althea looked embarrassed.

"And I know you hippie kids these days have loosey-goosey ideas about marriage. But, really Doc, wouldn't it be nice to have a big blowout wedding with your families attending? This island is a great place for a wedding and honeymoon. Let's fly in your families and I'll foot the bill for it all."

"But this is such short notice for everyone," Althea protested.

"Oh, take a few weeks to get it set up. Which brings up the next subject; I need a doctor."

The three were alarmed.

"Why? What's wrong?" Luke said, "You seem OK."

Hughes laughed.

"I feel better than I have for years thanks to Doc. No, I mean that I'm an old man with, I admit, some peculiar habits. I hate being around people, though you kids are OK, I guess. But I fall too easily into unhealthy behavior."

Yeah, obsessive-compulsive behavior, he thought. He remembered that, during their captivity, when he felt anxious, he would do repetitive, nit-picking acts, like re-arranging the silverware on the table, over and over. He sighed.

"I need someone I can trust. I want to hire you, Doc, as my personal physician."

Althea said sadly, "Howard, I ...". He held up a hand.

"I know you're not a headshrinker, Doc. And I'm ready to admit now, after almost dying in that quake, that maybe I could use the help of one. But you've got good intuition and you've helped me a lot so far."

"But I was offered a job in Detroit."

"You haven't accepted it yet, have you?"

"No, but ..."

"Look, Doc, you don't have to be full-time with me. Help me get medical and support staff that we both trust. I'm sure we can find you a job here on the island. I know they have clinics here that could always use doctors."

He tried hard not to sound like he was begging.

Harry said, "Althea, why not try it for a few weeks? I need to get back to Vegas and get things lined up there, with the casinos and with whatever staff Mr. Hughes has left. Luke needs to report back to his base, though I'm sure we can persuade them to give him a break for your wedding. You can help get Mr. Hughes settled in."

Althea was quiet. Howard tried to breath slowly, as she had taught him, to quell his anxiety

"OK," she said, "Two weeks here then off to Detroit." Howard felt a wave of relief. He turned, smiling.

"And Luke, I made a call this morning. You have one month to get ready for a meeting in California."

"Huh?" Luke replied brilliantly.

#

Luke stood nervously in the reception room at Hughes Aircraft. The walls were covered with plaques and photos detailing the history of the many projects produced there. He turned as a man entered the room.

"Lieutenant Priss?"

They shook hands. Pat Hyland, Vice President of Hughes Aircraft, was even older than Hughes and seemed a mild and affable man. But Luke had done his homework and knew that Hyland was a sharp engineer not prone to wasting time on silly ideas. They entered a conference room.

"Thanks for seeing me, Mr. Hyland," Luke said, "I'll try not to take too much of your time."

"Howard was very enthusiastic about your idea so I'm happy to hear about it."

This sounded nice enough but Luke thought that Hughes

had probably presented Hyland with a slew of concepts over the years, many of them impractical, half-baked, and quickly shot down. Luke needed to make his best case and had one chance to do it. Hughes' initial enthusiasm would not be enough.

Luke pulled a slide tray from his briefcase and loaded it into the projector on the table.

Hyland said, "Before you start, I have to ask you if you've applied for any patents on your concept."

Harry had insisted that Luke do so, saying that no corporation would even talk to him if it meant that he might sue them in the future for 'stealing' his idea, even if it was one they were already working on. A patent gave someone 'dibs' on an idea and so was protection for both parties.

"Yes," Luke said, pulling out a folder, "Here's a copy."

Hyland set it aside.

"OK, let's hear what you've got."

As he had with Hughes in the cockpit of the airplane, but in greater detail, Luke started with the financial aspects of building the small spaceship. Hyland listened quietly and said little. Luke moved onto the technical aspects. After a few minutes, Hyland stood up.

"Excuse me a minute," he said, and left the room.

Luke thought, *Damn it, that's it. He's not buying it. His secretary will be in soon to show me out, oh so politely. I blew it.*

Luke turned off the slide projector and sat waiting miserably. Hyland came back in with three men trailing him. Luke stood to meet them.

Hyland said, "Luke, these are some of our Senior Engineers. I'm sorry but can I ask you to start from the beginning? I want them to get all the details."

Luke grinned and spun the slide tray around to the first slide.

"Happy to."

The meeting went on for the rest of the morning. Hyland and his engineers bombarded Luke with questions.

"Why just rocket engines? Why not add jet engines to ferry the ship from factory to airport and so on?," one said.

"Weight savings. Jet engines would only work up to 50,000

feet or so and would be useless, dead weight for 90% of each launch. Yes, the seven rocket engines would use more propellant than jet engines when flying from airport to airport but the propellant cost is worth it for the increase in cargo to space."

Another engineer asked, "What about heat shielding?"

Luke admitted, "That is an area that will require more research. I'm thinking carbon/silica carbide but it is a bit heavy. As I said, needs more research."

Eventually, Hyland held up both hands and the conversation stopped. He said, "Well, I have a feeling this could go on for hours so let's make assignments, wrap it up, and schedule the next meeting. Guys, I want a rough estimate made of the design and development costs and schedule to present to Mr. Hughes. If he approves, we make it happen. Luke, I'll have our lawyers contact you to discuss a contract for your role in this project. It's going to need a name. Suggestions?"

Luke clicked to the last slide. It showed two photos; a KC-135 refueling a jet and a small bird hovering in flight, its long beak sipping nectar from a flower.

"I propose 'Hummingbird'".

Hyland said, "No objections? Then Project Hummingbird it is."

Chapter 20: Gateway

The wedding that June was beautiful. *Even nicer than my three weddings*, Howard thought. He watched the outdoor ceremony and reception from his penthouse balcony with binoculars and listened in with headphones and a parabolic 'spy ear' amplifier. He had met Althea's parents and was sure they thought he was an odd duck, to put it mildly. '*But hey*', he told himself, '*I think so too.*'

He watched Althea take the microphone and heard her say, "Luke and I would like to give our deepest thanks to Howard Hughes for his support and friendship. So, a toast."

They all turned to the balcony and raised their glasses.

"To Howard!"

He reflexively pulled back into the shadows, away from the gaze of dozens of people but still, somehow, felt pleased.

#

A week later, per Hughes' request, the four met again in his suite.

Hughes said, "I want to talk about our plans for the next few years. The Hummingbird ship won't be ready to fly for a couple of years. Last month, NASA launched their first crew to the Skylab space station. By this time next year, the third crew will have left the station and it will be sitting up there empty. As far as I can tell, there are no real plans by NASA to ever use it again. They've slowly started designing their Space Shuttle vehicle but Nixon decided against spending any money on a space station for the Shuttle to actually shuttle to and from. Maybe they'll build a station in a couple of decades."

Harry said, "Luke, remember your prediction when we first met? You were right. The government is winding the Space Program down to a bare-bones level. If you can call spending three billion dollars a year 'bare-bones'."

Luke said, "Oh, NASA will spend some of it on great science projects like unmanned probes to the planets but, yeah, I think most of it will go to support the Shuttle. And, despite hype

from NASA, I bet the Shuttle will only launch
maybe four or five times a year. So it will still be super-expensive
to put anything or anyone into space. I think NASA is mostly
trying to keep their engineers employed and hoping for better times
to come."

Hughes said, "So much for building a space-faring
civilization, eh?"

He let Luke, Althea, and Harry sit there glumly for a
minute then grinned at them. "You know, when I was your age
they put Flash Gordon and Buck Rogers space adventures in the
funny papers. I was a grown man by then and thought they were
pretty silly. But lately I've read stories that Doc told me about,
science fiction stories. I guess some of them are a step up from the
comic strips. That Robert Heinlein fellow seems to know a bit of
engineering, except when he has two guys building a spaceship in
their backyard. That's just silly. Though he's pretty good at
describing some futures that would be grand places to live in."

They stared at him.

Finally, Harry said, "Howard, you've lost me. What do
NASA projects have to do with Robert Heinlein stories?"

Hughes said, "Not much. Look, what I'm trying to say is
that you kids have gotten me interested in the future again. When I
was young, aviation was the hottest thing around. Some of us
knew it would change the world. It did. Now it looks to me like the
most exciting future for humans is in space. But I'm mostly a doer,
not a dreamer. So how do we, the four of us, make that future?"

Luke said, "Isn't that what we plan to do with
Hummingbird?"

"Sure, but that's only a piece of it. We have to have other
research done and other projects lined up before Hummingbird
makes orbit. NASA won't do it for us. So we have to ignore
NASA, except when we
can use them. We can be inspired by Heinlein's optimism but we
have to be hard-nosed about money and physics. Building his kind
of future will have to be done with many, many baby steps.
Hummingbird is only the first step."

"And what's the next step?" Luke asked.

"Sending you up to Skylab as the first private astronaut."

Once again the three stared at him, with wide eyes and their jaws literally hanging open, just a little, Hughes was amused to see. "If you three goldfish think about it a minute, it's actually a pretty reasonable idea. Luke gets practice working in zero-gee, on real space hardware, doing experiments that focus on humans living in space. We use what he learns to design the next space habitats. Or even hotels. We'll give Hummingbird someplace to go. And on from there, out into the Solar System. We shouldn't waste this opportunity, like Congress wasted the Moon landings."

Howard saw Althea watching Luke. He sat stiff and quiet. She turned to Howard. "Would Nixon and NASA really be willing to foot the bill for this?"

Hughes said, "Well, we would have to agree to perform some NASA experiments and maybe some student experiments as well as our own. I would have to pay for Luke's spacesuits and training and supplies, and so on. Also, NASA would cancel the Apollo-Soyuz mission and instead expect Luke to do some kind of joint stunt with the Commies. They'll be up there in their Salyut station for a while."

Harry said, "I remember that the agreement with the Russians says that orbital rendezvous 'is planned', so not absolutely committed to."

When the others stared at him, he said, "Hey, I like to keep up to date on the politics of space and the wording of these things is important."

Hughes said, "In any case, because of loans I made to Nixon's brother years ago I have some small leverage over the President. I just got his agreement to redirect the remaining Apollo hardware for our use, with some conditions. He'll also order the Air National Guard to assign Luke to NASA for training."

Howard was startled when Luke said angrily, with clenched jaw, "Shouldn't you have discussed all this with us first?"

Hughes snapped back, "I thought you'd jump at the chance! If you don't want to do it, I'm sure there are NASA astronauts already trained who'd love to go."

He glared at Luke who glared right back. Althea stood up. "Stop this," she said softly.

The men looked up at her.

She said gently, "Howard, this is a lot to take in. Let's all meet later for lunch after we've had time to think about it." He nodded.

Althea and Luke retreated to their suite. She closed the door gently behind them.

"Christ," said Luke, "He thinks he can play us like chess pieces."

"Come sit with me?" Althea said, going to the balcony. They sat and looked out at the ocean together.

"Luke, what's really going on?"

"I just don't like being manipulated."

"Yes, I imagine that being in the military, that must be annoying."

"That's different!"

"Is it? You joined the Guard for your own purpose, to learn to fly, so you put up with taking orders." She paused a beat. "Can I say what I think is really happening between you and Howard?"

"All right."

"You and I and Harry share a nerdy passion for great science fiction stories and for building a future inspired by those stories. It's a strong bond between us."

"True."

"Now Howard wants to join the party and you, another alpha male, feel like he's intruding into our happy family."

Luke was silent.

Althea said, "I guess I've always loved the shared joy at science fiction conventions. It's a big tent. Room for black women doctors, honest lawyers, hot-shot pilots and crazy old billionaires, if we could ever get him to go to one. But, if it matters, you're the man I want to share any future with, whether it's spectacular or a total dud. I will always be on your side, flyboy." Luke was quiet.

Althea said, "You really want to go to Skylab, don't you?"

Luke said, "Yep. I do."

Althea sighed. "It would be cool," she said. *And dangerous,* she thought.

Luke said, "But I won't. Not without you."

Althea laughed. "You can't believe that NASA would send

me up with you! I'm a doctor, not an astronaut."

Luke nodded. "True," he said, "You know, after the earthquake, I thought I'd lost you forever. Now that I've got you back, I can't imagine being separated for months of training and mission. I want to be next to you every night, even with the snoring."

"Wait, what?"

"So I'm asking you to look for a job at a hospital in Las Vegas, at least unti I finish my tour of duty in the Air National Guard. Howard can find another guy for the mission. We'll still learn a lot to help with future projects and..."

"But you really want to go, don't you?" she said.

Luke sighed. "It would be so cool," he said. Althea nodded.

"OK, how about this?" she said, "We would need a team of experts to help with the mission. Why don't I join that team? To help with any medical issues, collect data. I could be with you during the training period at least."

"Would you be willing to do that?"

"Yes. You being in space, alone in a big tin can, scares me, I admit. You have to promise me to be super careful. No unnecessary risk taking, OK?"

"I promise," Luke said, getting up and taking her hand, "I'll be a careful guinea pig. Let's go tell Howard and Harry that I'm good to go."

Althea shook her head, stood, and moved to him.

"Lunch is a couple hours away, husband. They can wait."

Luke smiled and took her in his arms.

Chapter 21: The Postman

A knock on the door. FBI Special Agent Susan Roley, Omaha Office, looked up from her desk as her boss entered her tiny office. He handed her a large binder. "Roley, this came in the mail today. It's probably a prank from some nutjob. You get to deal with it."

Susan sighed. As one of the first two female Special Agents in the FBI, she was still proving herself and was usually given the less-interesting assignments.

"Right."

Her boss left. Susan reached into a drawer, found some white cotton gloves, and put them on. Then she opened the three-ring binder, trying to just touch the edges. She hoped her boss had not already smeared any possible fingerprints. The first page was a letter to the FBI. It had no social niceties like "Dear FBI" but simply read:

"A series of bombs is being distributed. The attached Manifesto will explain why. I have sent a copy of my Manifesto and other material to the New York Times. They must publish all that I send them or I will keep adding bombs to the series. The other material I have sent you and the Times is a set of encrypted messages. Each message describes the destination and specific reason for a particular bomb but can't be decoded and read without its own special numerical key. Once a bomb detonates, and that fact is printed in the New York Times, I will call your office with the key for that message. This will verify that I was the source of the bomb. Also, Agent Insert-Name-Here, I have sent a duplicate of this package to another FBI office. So if you do not take me seriously, perhaps they will. Enjoy."

Susan sat and thought for a moment. She called the Forensics Department. "I need to have fingerprints, hair samples, etc taken from an item in my office ASAP. Room B217. Right. See you soon."

She called her boss. "The binder you left me must have been wrapped for delivery, right? Can you get me that wrapping material? I want to have it checked by Forensics. OK, thanks."

Susan called other FBI offices to ask if they had

received a similar package. Finally, she got a positive from the head of the Saint Louis office.

"Yeah, I just assigned that to Agent Pierce," he said.

Susan smiled. Agent Joanne Pierce was the only other female Special Agent in the FBI. FBI Director J. Edgar Hoover had forbidden female agents but he died and the Bureau had moved with the times. She and Susan had gone through training together in Quantico, Virginia.

"Thanks. I'll give her a call."

Joanne picked up on the first ring. "Agent Pierce."

"Hey Sister, how's it hanging?"

"Sue!" Joanne laughed, "Hey, I left the convent years ago. It's Special Agent now, thank you very much."

Susan said, "They dumped The Math Bomber case on you, did they?"

"Ah, so your Office got the other package. Is that what we're going to call this case, the Math Bomber? Checking the package and binder for evidence?" Joanne said.

"You bet. Forensics should be here soon."

Susan used tweezers to grip the pages so she wouldn't smear any fingerprints. She flipped to the back of the binder. "Did you see in the back, the sheets of numbers?"

"Yes, those must be his encoded messages," Joanne said. "We'd better bring in the guys in the Cryptanalysis and Racketeering Unit. They should have fun with those. He even gives instructions on how to decode each message, once he gives us the key."

"And why do you think he's doing that? Just to taunt us?" said Susan.

"Sure. If he's trying to do a campaign of terror, looking in complete control helps his cause. Notice that he sent a copy of the whole package to the New York Times. If they publish the coded messages, there will be a frenzy in the public to decode them. Great publicity for him and his cause," Joanne said.

"And if no one can crack the codes, it makes him look like a genius, us look impotent, and, again, helps his cause. As well as making the public feel helpless."

"Exactly," Joanne said, "So we need to impress urgency on

the Cryptanalysis boys, before bombs start going off."

"Unless this guy is just a crank," said Susan.

"I pray that he is."

"Amen, Sister."

Chapter 22: Inheritance

In his office at the back of *The Lucky Leprechaun* casino, Mike Remains laid the box, wrapped in brown paper and postmarked Spokane, Washington, on his desk. His son Harry sat across from him, raising his eyebrows in silent inquiry.

"The postman just handed me this, as it would not fit in our mailbox," Mike said. He pushed it to one side.

"Son, we need to talk about these loans Howard Hughes has offered us that you've refused to take. Why?"

Harry held up a hand and began ticking off on his fingers, "One, we don't need them to expand or improve our casino. Two, Howard likes to control everything. These loans would be a wedge to eventually take us over. Three, I manage the managers of his casinos in Vegas. If I got special treatment, it makes them resent me and so makes my job harder. So, no."

Mike sighed. "Alright. We'll play it your way for now, son."

"Thanks, Da," Harry said as he left the office.

Mike pulled the package over and got out a letter opener. Harry was down the hall when the bomb went off.

Chapter 23: The Dispossessed

August, 1973

Luke was in a locker room at Cape Kennedy. A technician was helping him suit up for a training session in the Apollo Simulator. Deke Slayton, the Director of Flight Crew Operations, came in and locked eyes with Luke. "Meet me in my office when you're done."

"Yes, sir." Deke left.

The techie said, "Hoo-ee, that should be a fun conversation. You know he was slated to fly the Apollo-Soyuz mission when your mission bumped his?"

Luke nodded.

The tech went on, "Heart issue kept him on the bench until recently. He's never been in space. Now he may never get to go up."

Luke sighed. There were some at NASA who resented him, this stranger coming out of left field, buying his way to space with a billionaire's money. All he could do, he thought, was focus on the mission and ignore the barbs. Soon he was climbing into the Apollo simulator, a huge, boiler-plate conical module. The techs ran him through one scenario after another, giving him simulated system failures to deal with, fuel leaks, communication losses, the whole nine yards. He had been doing this for hours every day, until he thought he could run the controls with his eyes closed. Finally he finished, cleaned up, and reported to Deke's office.

"Major," said Luke, as he saluted.

Deke waved him to take a seat then gazed at him with a stony expression and steely eyes. Luke nervously wondered if that was a mixed metaphor.

"Priss, I don't like your mission."

Luke said nothing.

"And not for the reason you think."

"Sir?"

"I don't like it because it's badly designed," Deke went on, "You're one man going to a space station designed to be maintained by three. The first crew had a hell of a time getting the station operational after it was damaged in launch and the second crew just went up."

Deke got up and paced the room as he continued.

"Next year you're going up alone with a pile of equipment that has not been adequately tested by NASA. You have your own staff of engineers recruited from God knows where. Your boss is a crazy hermit who treats NASA like we're his private taxi service. Your team isn't sharing information on your planned experiments or even mission duration. The whole thing is way too sloppy," Deke finished.

"That's a long list, sir. What changes do you suggest?"

Deke gave Luke a sour look. "First, *you*, not Howard Hughes, need to take command of the mission. It's your ass on the line, not his. You need to trust NASA more, even if there may be some here who feel threatened by the so-called 'private space' paradigm you and Hughes represent. Bring your pack of engineers here, we'll find a space for them to work. Share information on your equipment and experiments. Believe it or not, we work with private contractors all the time and know how to respect confidentiality."

"Can I work with you on setting all that up, sir?"

"Sure. Since you guys destroyed the Apollo-Soyuz mission, I find I have more time on my hands."

Luke flushed.

Deke grinned. "I'm just messing with you, Priss. Dismissed."

"Yes, sir. Thank you, sir."

Chapter 24: Ender's Game

During spring break, Ted rented a car and drove west. He told the Principal that he was visiting old friends and would stop in at Las Vegas 'for a bit of fun'.

"Don't bet more than you're willing to lose, Carl," said the Principal, with a wink.

"Oh, if there's one thing I've learned in life, it's how to reduce my risks and always have a backup plan."

When he got to Vegas he mailed another set of packages. He couldn't do it back in Butte; the Post Office clerk there knew him and if the FBI could identify the postmarks on any of the bomb remnants, they might find him. While in Vegas, he drove past The Lucky Leprechaun. With great satisfaction, he saw the 'Closed' sign in the parking lot.

Not so lucky now, are you, you son of a bitch?

He drove on to the post office to mail the packages. He had, as always, carefully cleaned them so there were no fingerprints or even stray hairs that could possibly be traced back to him.

#

Special Agent Roley was having a hard day. A sixth bomb had gone off, this one at the Indian Springs Air Base in Nevada. It had killed the commander of the base. The New York times reported on it and, within hours, a phone call came to the Omaha office.

"To the Agent dealing with the recent explosion at Indian Springs Air Base," said the man's voice.

He then slowly and clearly provided a 20 digit number, repeated it once, and hung up. There was no way to trace the call in the short time he was connected. The recorded message was sent up to Roley's office. She listened carefully, writing down the number. Then she called the Crypto boys and passed it on to them. After three bombs had gone off they were finally allowed to buy an IBM 360 computer, the first computer used in their department. Using the software provided with the Manifesto and the 20 digit key from the phone call, they were able to decrypt the next message attached to the Manifesto. They sent the text on to Roley and to Pierce, her partner in the investigation. Per the Math Bomber's demand, the FBI passed all decrypted messages on to the New York Times. Roley hated that. It simply helped build the Bomber's reputation of invincibility. But her higher-ups took seriously his threat to add more bombs if they didn't cooperate.

That afternoon Roley had a visitor.

"Mr. Remains, first, I want to say that I am so sorry for the loss of your father."

"Thank you, Agent Roley. I appreciate that," said Harry, "But what I need, what my family needs, is for you to catch the bastard. I know this is an ongoing case and that limits what you can share with me. But I may be able to provide useful information."

"What kind of information?"

"A possible suspect."

"I'm listening."

"First, a question: do you think the bomb that killed my father was sent by the so-called Math Bomber?" Harry asked.

"Yes, he even gave us the key to decode the message connected to it."

"Didn't you find that his reason given in that message for bombing a small casino was rather lame? I mean, 'representatives of corrupt consumer capitalism'?" Harry asked, "If that was his actual motivation he would have hit a big name casino, like Caesar's Palace. So why my family's business?"

"Are you saying it was personal?"

"Exactly. I think he's the so-called 'UGLi Bomber' that my friend Luke Priss and I helped capture in '69. He's mailed six bombs so far but one was to my family's casino, one to the air base Luke is stationed at, and one to The Xanadu Princess Hotel to Howard Hughes. That one killed his secretary. Hughes is my boss and is also financing a project Luke created."

"Yes, I'm familiar with the 'UGLi Bomber' case. Even though he was incarcerated he was one of the first suspects we checked out since he had a PhD in math. One problem: he's dead. Killed in an explosion at his prison in '72," said Roley.

"And I'm suggesting that he did not die, that he faked it

somehow and escaped. I can't see the police records from that episode but you can. I'm just asking you to look into the possibility."

Roley saw the desperation in Harry's face.

What the hell, we don't have any other leads.

"All right , Mr. Remains, we'll look into that. But I can't say I'll be able to share any results with you."

"That's OK, Agent Roley. Thanks for hearing me out."

Harry stood and shook her hand. Roley thought he still looked grief-stricken but also like a bit of guilt had been taken from his burden. Guilt that his capture of the UGLi Bomber had led to pain for his family. He closed the office door quietly behind him. Roley pulled a file out and called Agent Pierce.

Chapter 25: Dangerous Visions

September, 1974

One of Ted's students came into his room early on the first day of class.

"Mr. Frikes! Hi!"

"Hello Billy, how was your summer?"

"Great! But I wanted to show you this magazine my Dad gave me. It's called 'Physics Today' and it has a really cool article about space colonies!"

Ted blinked. *More high tech bullshit.*

"That's fine, Billy, but class is starting in a few minutes so..."

"Right! I'll just leave it with you. I'd really like to talk with you about it soon!"

That evening, while eating a TV dinner in his tiny kitchen, Ted read the article by Princeton physicist Gerard O'Neill. It infuriated him. He wanted to tear the magazine to shreds but remembered Billy. *Have to maintain mellow Mr. Frikes for the little brats.*

O'Neill made a case for building free-floating rotating space colonies, the size of cities but in orbit, not on the surface of any planet or moon. Miles across, the interior environment would be like the most pleasant parts of Earth. Ted was not an engineer but, after running some of O'Neill's equations on his calculator, he had to admit that O'Neill's math seemed to make sense. But that meant that the human race could spread out into the Solar System within decades, using solar energy and resources from the Moon and asteroids. Then there would be no stopping the growth of technology.

Ted paced back and forth in his small living room. The more he thought about space settlements, the more agitated he became. His hands were shaking so hard he almost dropped the magazine. O'Neill wanted to spread plant, animal, and human life out into a lifeless Solar System. In Ted's mind, the worst possible outcome. Humans were a cancer on the Earth. They could not be allowed to metastasize. To save the planet, hell, the universe, the human species must be humbled and brought back to a hunter-gatherer existence. Ted took a deep breath to calm himself. *This changes things. This changes everything.*

The next day, an excited Billy ran up to Ted. "Mr. Frikes, did you have a chance to read the article?"

"Yes, Billy. It gave me a lot to think about. Thanks. Maybe we'll talk about it sometime."

Ted was genuinely grateful to Billy. The space colonization concept gave Ted a new focus. Ted had seen himself as one soldier in the battle for the planet. He had been under no illusion that he alone could save the planet. He had hoped to inspire more eco-terrorists with his Manifesto while also eliminating a few technocrat monsters. But thinking beyond the surface of one little blue planet gave him a new perspective and a new plan.

Getting into space currently was hard and expensive so only two countries so far bothered sending people to space. Public support in the United States for human space travel was shrinking. Other countries seemed to promote humans in space only in competition with the US. All well and good. But there were plans to make space travel cheaper, which might lead to projects like O'Neill's space settlements. So if Ted could strike at key points in the US space program, just enough to slow projects down, costs would go up and projects might be canceled. Other nations would be under less pressure to compete As the environment on Earth deteriorated, there would be even less public support to go off-planet. Humans would stay trapped on one planet, stewing in their own pollution and over-population, eventually collapsing back to a more sustainable, some would say primitive, way of life. Ted's efforts would now be completely focused on stopping space travel. *Focused like a laser*, he told himself with a little laugh.

Ted spent the next month making a new series of bombs, picking targets, and forming a new list of encrypted messages, one for each bomb. *Oh dear*, he thought, *I've almost run through the old series of bombs. And I did promise the FBI I would only add bombs if they didn't share my messages with the press.* He laughed. *Screw 'em.*

Ted bicycled to the Butte Post Office with a package. Like all the others he had sent, it was wrapped in plain brown paper, but unlike the others, had a return address of 'Carl Frikes, Butte Montana High School, 3225 Wharton St., Butte, Montana 59701'. He had high hopes for its contents. Very high hopes.

Chapter 26: Cosmic Engineers

The two women and five men walked into the large room in the Manned Spacecraft Operations Building at NASA.

"Our new home," said George, a big, bearded redhead.

Peter, a short, balding mechanical engineer, said "I call a window desk," though the room was windowless.

Peter was odd but not unusual for the collection. Billie Burke, a petite blond software engineer, glanced around. "Good. Plenty of wall space for cork or blackboards," she said. "And it's right next to the workshop for you Oompa Loompas to build your toys."

The others set down their load of boxes.

"Geez, that was a long walk," said Hans.

"So let's move the van to this end of the building and snag a dolly from the workshop," said Freeman.

The Team spanned a wide range of technical and scientific skills. Howard Hughes, Luke, Althea, and Harry had each suggested people to recruit and agreed on the name for the group. The Team members were respected in their fields but also known to be creative and willing to challenge the status quo. Maybe it wasn't a coincidence but most of them were also science fiction fans. Althea and Harry had met a number of them at conventions and were comfortable with them. Peter had wanted to call the group 'The Mercurial Seven' because he claimed some members had hair-trigger tempers. They didn't, though he did sometimes try their patience.

They were getting settled in to their new digs when Luke stopped by. "Hey guys," he said, "Welcome to Florida. It's good to finally see us all together. All but Althea."

"Yeah Luke," said Peter, "When does our Chief Medical Officer join us?"

"I'm going to get her at the airport now. She's taken a leave from her hospital on Grand Bahama Island for the duration of this mission. We'll go see about renting an apartment and then I'll bring her here to join you. Save her a good desk."

Luke saw Billie Burke squint her eyes and purse her lips as if something concerned her but he was anxious to see

Althea and didn't ask Billie what was on her mind. He left quickly and drove to the airport in his old red and white Thunderbird. Waiting for Althea by the luggage carousel, he saw her exiting the gate area, looking nervous, clutching her purse to her chest. Luke's heart sent a warm rush through him at the sight of her. Luke strode up to her smiling, with arms out-stretched for a big hug. Althea held up one hand, as if to ward him off. "Sorry Luke, later OK?" she said.

Luke was hurt but didn't push it. He turned his energy to snagging her luggage from the carousel and carrying it to the car. After they got in, he took her hand. "Darlin', is something wrong?"

Althea squeezed his hand and gave him a tight-lipped smile. "Sorry Luke, I just feel self-conscious being with you in a sea of white folks. This isn't Detroit or Grand Bahama Island. Maybe I just notice the stares more than you do."

As they drove to the apartment building, he said,"Honey, I think you'll like this place. It's a nice two bedroom apartment with lots of windows. The landlady was pretty excited to get an astronaut tenant."

"And how did she feel about an astronaut's black wife?"
Luke was silent.
"Damn it, Luke, you didn't tell her?"
"Honey, she seemed very nice…."
Althea just shook her head. When they entered the office to meet the landlady, Althea saw her face freeze at the sight of a black woman. *And here we go*, Althea thought. She could almost see the gears turning in the woman's brain.

Luke said, "Mrs. Brody, this is my wife Althea. I'd like her to see the apartment you showed me yesterday."

"Oh, gosh," Mrs. Brody stammered. "That apartment isn't available anymore. Uh, there was a small fire and it'll take months to repair."

Althea turned to the door. "Let's go Luke."
Luke looked at her, startled. "But.."
"No. We are leaving. Now," said Althea.
She got into the car and sat staring straight ahead. Luke got in and said, "I'm sure we'll find something. We just have to keep looking."

She turned and glared at him. "Really?" she snapped, "Luke, if I were white or you were black, maybe we could. But this is the Deep South, the Deepest. Our marriage wasn't even legal here just six years ago. And Florida didn't make it legal, the Supreme Court had to do it. I think you're being damned naive. I just hope your motel lets me through the door."

They drove in silence back to NASA. When they walked into the office, The Team moved to greet them warmly but Billie Burke saw that they were upset. "Appointment didn't go so well?" she asked.

"No," said Luke, "I was an idiot."

Althea touched his arm sympathetically but didn't contradict him.

"Yes, I thought you might meet some resistance," said Billie, "Look, we," she waved a hand at the others, "all live at the same hotel. I took the liberty and made some calls. There is a nice suite waiting for you two."

Althea raised an eyebrow. "Really? Is the manager aware of our melanin distribution issue?"

Billie grinned. "Oh yes but I called the owner of the building and he vouched for both of you to the manager."

Luke said, "The owner? Who…?"

Althea smiled, "Howard!"

"Yep!" said Billie. "He had agreed with me that The Team should all live close to each other, to brainstorm. He knows that creative types don't turn it off at the end of the work day. I think he sees it as a way to get free labor. Only natural to include you two."

"Yay!" said Peter, "Problem solved. Big group hug!" Everybody scattered.

#

Weeks later, Peter and Luke stood in the huge workshop. The floor was largely taken up by Peter's creation, a twenty-two foot diameter ring of cables, metal struts, and motors, laying on its three-foot-wide edge.

Peter said, "So you'll install this centrifuge inside Skylab right next to the ring of lockers that run around the circular wall.

You'll have to assemble it the first or second day you enter the station because we don't want the rabbits, chickens, or plants growing in zero gravity any longer than that. Rachel says it would mess up the gestation data."

Skylab had been made from a huge cylindrical fuel tank, the size of a house, from a leftover Saturn V rocket. Luke knew that the current Skylab crew members would, just for fun, run in circles inside the station around the ring of storage lockers. Centrifugal force would press their feet against the lockers so they looked like big hamsters racing in a wheel. In Luke's case, he would be installing an actual wheel spanning the width of the station. Motors would spin it to provide centrifugal force pseudo-gravity for anything or anyone riding inside the ring.

Peter said, "It'll spin at a bit less than five seconds for each revolution. This will make a gravity level about 65% of Earth's on the floor of the centrifuge where we'll have cages for some of the chickens and rabbits. Hopefully they will breed so we can see if fetuses develop OK at that gravity level. Can't have space settlements if we can't have babies, right? We also made a place in the wheel for a pad for you to sleep on. You get to be one of the experiments. You'll store periodic urine samples so we can see if 65% gravity is enough to reduce the negative effects of zero g on the human body, like bone loss. We also have shelves four feet above the floor of the centrifuge for some of your plants and animals. Being closer to the center of rotation, they'll feel a Martian gravity level, 38% of Earth's. More shelves will be eight feet above the floor to provide a Lunar gravity level."

Luke said, "I see it's got three motors to drive it at the rim. What happens if one burns out? Can the other two keep it up to speed, even when it has to carry my mass and all the experiments? We don't want to have to stop it for repairs and expose any of the critters to zero-gee unnecessarily."

"Sure, no problem. Even one motor can keep the ring spinning.," said Peter, "But you'll have three spare motors and you can replace a bad one without stopping the spinning ring."

"What about me getting into and out of the ring? How is that going to affect the balance of the centrifuge?"

Peter pointed. "See those two crossbars running across the

ring, one on either face, forming a big 'X'? They'll each hold a tank of water that motors will move along the crossbar automatically to keep the ring in balance."

Luke pointed to the backup Skylab looming in the other end of the workshop. It was a duplicate of the actual orbiting space station and was going to be moved to the Smithsonian Air and Space Museum in a few months.

"I want the centrifuge disassembled and all the components packed as they will be in the Command Module. I need to practice moving them into the backup Station and assembling them in place. Obviously doing it in zero-gee will be very different from doing it here but, if we need to redesign any parts, we'd better do it now."

Peter stood at attention, clicked his heels, saluted, and said, "Mai oui, mon Capitan. It shall be done."

#

Months later, the day before launch, Deke called Althea and Luke into his office. "Luke, I don't think we can squeeze any more training into that thick head of yours. Tomorrow's going to be a busy, long day for all of us so you and Althea get out of here. Try to get to sleep early. See you at 5am tomorrow."

"Thanks Deke," said Luke.

Chapter 27: Mission of Gravity

May 12, 1975

Luke rode the elevator up the launch tower with two techs. The Saturn 1B was less than half the height of the mighty moon-launching Saturn V but still more than ten stories tall. Luke strode along the catwalk to the Apollo capsule. The techs opened the hatch, helped Luke squeeze in, and strapped him into the center seat of the capsule. The other two seats had been removed to make space for all the hardware and livestock he was bringing to Skylab. The hatch closed. The rabbits were silent in their cages but the chickens made low 'awww' sounds. The place smelled like a pet shop. Luke waited patiently, almost dozing. Finally….

"T-minus 1 minute," said Deke in Luke's earpiece. The Team sat in the Control Room and watched on the big screen. Only Althea and Billie had seats in front of monitors, Billie to deal with software issues and Althea to track Luke's vital signs.

Hunched over the screen, she noted that his pulse rate and respiration were normal. Althea knew that, like Neil 'Iceman' Armstrong, Luke would stay calm in a stressful situation. *Not like me.* She sat straighter, lowered her shoulders, and took deep breaths, trying to relax. *Now if only the damned rocket works.*

"...3, 2, 1, we have liftoff!," said Deke.

The Saturn 1B slowly rose from the launch pad. Deke could hear the engines rumbling through Luke's mike. But he also heard a high-pitched keening sound. "Luke, we're getting an odd high frequency sound."

"That's the rabbits. They're freaking out. But the chickens seem pretty calm."

The acceleration grew. Luke was pressed hard into his seat. He kept his breathing slow and deep. Zero to 60 in a few seconds, he thought. But, unlike a fast sports car, the pressure went on and on. A couple minutes later he felt the jolt as the 1st stage, now depleted, dropped from the rocket. A few seconds of feeling like falling off a cliff. Then another kick as the second stage engines ignited. Eight minutes later the engines cut out and he again felt the weird lightness of free fall. Luke was in space. But three hours later he had still not reached Skylab.

#

Rachel the biologist entered the Control Room and took an observer's seat near Billie and Althea. She frowned.

"Why is he not there yet? Did something go wrong?"

Billie glanced at Althea and saw her stiffen. Billie glared at Rachel. "Actually, he's doing fine. It usually takes hours to rendezvous in orbit. You have to match location, speed, and direction, all while conserving fuel. He's doing fine," Billie repeated.

Luke's voice came over the speakers. "Station in view and closing."

The Team cheered. Deke Slayton held up a hand to shush them.

"We copy, Skylab 5."

Luke made it look easy. Billie had played on the simulator and knew how hard it could be to dock the Command Service Module to the station. She failed many more times than she succeeded. But Luke was like your annoying friend who can parallel park a car perfectly in one smooth move. The Command Module slipped into the port with barely a bump.

"Clamps engaged," Luke reported.

This time Deke let the Control Room cheer. Billie and Althea hugged with relief. "Well," said Billie, "He's definitely not in Kansas anymore."

#

Luke opened the hatch leading to the interior of the station. The air was warm and musty. It smelled like a locker room, even after a year since the last mission. Luke started to unload the Command Service Module. The rabbits and chickens were not happy and fussed as he clipped their cages to the walls of the station.

"I'm working on it guys. Hang tight," he said to the animals.

"Repeat Skylab 5. We did not copy," said Deke.

"Just calming the livestock, Control."

Luke went through all the systems on the station. Fuel cell reserves, water and air supplies, CO2 scrubbers, solar panel power output. All were good to go. He quickly shed his space suit so he could work more easily in a blue jumpsuit. He unloaded the centrifuge components from the CSM and carried them to the middle of the station. He flew like Superman, another orphan from Kansas, with a bundle under one arm and the other arm stretched out before him. It felt great.

The interior felt much bigger than the duplicate backup station back home. He could move easily anywhere in the big volume and wasn't confined to the grid floor that bisected the station. He assembled the color-coded parts of the centrifuge and bolted them to the circular wall of the station, right next to the ring of storage lockers. Other Skylab astronauts had advised him that losing small objects was one of their biggest headaches, as parts and tools drifted away in zero-gee to who-knew-where. Luke had magnetic patches sewn onto the upper legs of his jumpsuit. They held the small fasteners he needed. He had the centrifuge assembled in a couple of hours.

"Control, ready to spin up the centrifuge."

"Copy."

Luke flipped the switch on the wall and the centrifuge lurched and squealed as it slowly began turning. Luke turned the power off. "Needs tweaking."

It took another two hours of tightening and adjusting cables and motors before Luke was satisfied. The centrifuge ring now spun quietly and smoothly.

"Last test," said Luke.

He floated to just outside the center of the turning centrifuge and grabbed one of the cross bars spanning its width. The motors easily kept the ring turning once every four and a half seconds. He slowly pulled himself toward one end of the crossbar. As he spun around, centrifugal force pulled his feet toward the floor of the ring. He moved slowly to step inside the ring. Motors moved a counter-weight along the crossbar, away from Luke, to balance his mass. Funny, being in zero-gee had not been a problem for him but spinning around in a glorified merry-go-round was making him a bit nauseous. He slowly lay down on the flat area that would serve as his bed and breathed deeply.

"Skylab 5, report," said Deke in his earpiece.

"Little queasy. Letting myself get used to the spinning. Seems worse when I move my head around."

He kept a barf-bag close at hand but, luckily, didn't need to use it. The centrifuge didn't simulate full Earth gravity; just about 2/3. So he felt light and pretty comfortable on the thin sleeping pad. He felt like closing his eyes and taking a nap but his work was far from done. He slowly sat up and climbed back up to the center of the centrifuge, giving the counter-weights time to match his movement. Then he pushed off back into the zero-gee of the station.

"Now installing livestock."

"Copy."

A tall rack spanned the twenty-two foot diameter of the centrifuge. Luke unclipped the rabbit and chicken cages one by one from the wall of the station and installed them into the rack. One hen cage and one female rabbit cage went onto the bottom of the rack near the floor of the centrifuge where they would live and breed at 2/3 Earth gravity. He put another pair of cages higher up, at the Martian gravity level. Then a set eight feet from the floor, at the lunar gravity level. Finally Luke placed the cages with the male rabbit and bantam rooster at the lowest level.

"Control, livestock in place, continuing to unload supplies."

He moved back to the Command Service Module and unloaded the animal feed. The boxes held dozens of small paper packets of carefully measured portions of Purina chicken and rabbit chow. He also brought in his own food supplies and personal items, but left the student experiments in the CSM for now. He was getting tired and there was no immediate need to move them. He went to use the zero-gee toilet where he found a note from the last crew.

It read, "Hey Luke, we figured you would find this note by the process of elimination."

Engineer humor, he thought. The note went on, "We've

hidden three gifts for you around the Station. Here's your first clue: Kali would approve." It was signed by Carr, Pogue, and Gibson, the crew members from the Skylab 4 mission. *Nice. Thanks guys.*

Luke decided to pursue the hidden treasures the next day. He was just too tired. He pocketed the note, cleaned up, then had a meal at the dining table in zero-gee. He had to move spoonfuls of the sticky food slowly toward his mouth so it wouldn't drift away.

This is going to get real old real fast.

He'd have to come up with a little dining area in the centrifuge. He slowly climbed back onto his sleeping pad and clipped his photo of Althea to the inside of the centrifuge so he could see her as he went to sleep and when he awoke.

"OK Control, I'm going to turn in now."

"Hold on for one minute, Luke."

#

Deke stood up and moved to Althea's station. She looked up questioningly.

"Doctor, would you come with me please?" said Deke.

She followed him into a small office. He gestured at a desk that held a microphone and headphones. "We've set up a private line for you and Luke. When his workday is done, you two can stay in touch. That switch will notify Luke that you're online. Goodnight Doctor."

Her eyes softened in gratitude. "Thank you Deke."

He closed the door behind him. Althea pressed the button.

"Attention, Space Cadet Priss. Do you copy?"

"Althea? Have you mutinied and taken command?"

"I wish. No, Deke was sweet enough to give us a private line to use in your off-hours. How are you feeling?"

Luke wondered just how private the line was. Deke could be recording everything to track his state of mind over time. What the hell, he just let himself relax into it.

"Tired. Ready for sleep but this centrifuge hums and clicks like I'm riding a train. I expect I'll get used to it. How are you doing, darlin'?"

"Fine now. At launch, I was scared. I had to keep reminding myself that nine guys got to Skylab before you and they're all home safe and sound. But I miss you."

They talked quietly a bit more.

"Flyboy, I'm going to let you sleep now. I love you."

"Love you too, Darlin'. I'll see you tomorrow."

#

Luke closed the connection. The lights in the station were on constantly for safety's sake so he put on a sleepmask. He lay back and was out in seconds.

Chapter 28: The Food of the Gods

May 13, 1975

Humming to himself, Luke moved on to check out the rest of the station systems. All were nominal, with oxygen, water, etc being at levels the last crew had reported as they exited the station. Thinking of the last crew, Luke unfolded the note he had found in the restroom. 'Kali would approve', the clue on it read. Kali. That sounded familiar. Luke remembered reading a novel by Roger Zelazny called 'Lord of Light'. In the story, colonists on an alien world recreated themselves as the pantheon of Hindu gods. It was a bit more fantasy than science fiction for his tastes but Althea liked it so he gave it a try. One of the characters was the Hindu goddess Kali. Often depicted with blue skin and many arms. Arms. Where on the station were arms? There were his own two arms, the arms of his spare jumpsuits, the arms on his spacesuit. And on the suits left by the last crew.

Luke found the old spacesuits clamped to the wall of the station. He poked around inside them until he felt something in the right sleeve of Carr's spacesuit. He pulled it out. It was a copy of Playboy magazine, October 1973 issue. He looked at the cover of the magazine. *Oh boy, an article by Gore Vidal. Can't wait to read that. Thanks guys.* But first, as probably all readers would, he opened to the centerfold. A second note floated out. He snagged it and put the Playboy on his sleeping pad in the centrifuge for later study before he read the note.

'This one will require an exhaustive search! After using it, you may want to cool your jets!' So.... something to do with exhausts? Rocket exhaust? Luke couldn't believe they would hide something inside an exhaust nozzle of one of the maneuvering engines outside the ship. It must be inside Skylab. There were fans to circulate air but nothing one would call an exhaust fan. The old crew wouldn't want him to stumble on their surprises so it must be somewhere or in something he would not be expected to use on his mission, like the old spacesuits left by the last crew. Luke glided up and down the eighty foot length of the station, spinning slowly while he speculated on hiding places. The search couldn't require that he simply tear through every nook and cranny in the house-sized station. A brute force approach like that would not be an elegant solution. Not that he thought of Pogue, Carr, and Gibson as all that elegant, but still, Luke wanted to respect the scavenger hunt process.

On his third pass gliding through Skylab, he stopped in front of the Astronaut Propulsion Unit clamped to the wall. This was an experimental backpack gadget that an astronaut might wear outside the station, floating in free space. It had a tank of nitrogen gas and hand controls so the user could fire bursts of gas to propel them in different directions. It had never been used outside the station and only gently tested inside the cavernous workshop. But it did have exhaust nozzles. He peered into them and spied something jammed into one. He pulled out a bottle of Tabasco hot sauce. *Cool! I mean hot!* Zero gravity tended to make astronauts feel congested so their sense of taste was dulled. Some complained that the food provided by NASA was just too bland. *This'll improve my menu a lot.*

A third note was wrapped around the bottle. Luke stashed the hot sauce in the kitchen then read the note: 'Your last gift from the Three Wise Guys: Take a note from Kepler's Magnum Opus. Also, take care of yourself Luke (with a little help from your friends).'

Luke was vaguely familiar with the astronomer Johannes Kepler but had no idea what his Magnum Opus might be. Luke spent the day doing chores and running experiments and let the clue marinate in the back of his mind. He had found in the past that sometimes ignoring a problem for a while would let a possible solution float to the surface. But at the end of the day he had nothing. When he woke the next day, still nothing. He really wanted to solve the puzzle on his own but decided he needed help. *Like the Three Wise Guys said, with a little help from my friends.* Luke called Control and asked for a meeting.

#

The Team was crowded into the little office that Althea

used for off-duty calls with Luke. A TV set up in the corner showed him floating near the station's dining table. "...so I know this problem is trivial but it's nagging at me," Luke finished.

Althea said, "And therefore is a distraction affecting the mission. Perfectly reasonable to spend work hours on it."

Luke chose to ignore the faint whiff of sarcasm. "Exactly," he said.

Rachel said, "So who is this Kepler again?" Half the Team groaned.

"17th century mathematician…," said Billie.

"Famous astronomer..," said Hans.

"Came up with laws of planetary motion that Isaac Newton would explain later.," said Freeman.

"But Magnum Opus is a musical term, isn't it?" said Luke.

"Usually, I guess," said Hans, "But Kepler thought the orbits of the planets really did correspond to musical intervals and really did generate music that we couldn't hear audibly but that our souls sorta kinda could."

"Weird," said Peter.

"Yeah but back in the 1600's, astrology and astronomy were equally respectable. Even Kepler made a living doing astrology though he really didn't think much of it," said Hans.

"So how does all this tie into the clue from the Three Wise Guys, 'Take a note from Kepler's Magnum Opus'?" asked Luke.

"Well 'note' does imply music and he did write up the idea of planetary music in a book, I think, but I have no idea what the title was. I guess we could try to find it?" said Hans.

"Hard to believe Gibson, Pogue, and Carr would make solving this puzzle so complicated," said Luke.

"Maybe they just wanted to remind you that you can't always solve problems on your own," Althea said gently.

"And sometimes not even with help," Luke said wryly.

They all sat quietly for a while, stuck for ideas.

Finally, Rachel said, "You know, I always thought the phrase 'Music of the Spheres' was a poetic expression. No idea it might have come from an astronomer."

Luke laughed. "Bingo! Spheres!"

Rachel looked confused. "What spheres?"

Luke said, "Hold on, guys. I'll be right back." He jumped away from the table in the dining room and flew through the opening of the floor-grid between the two halves of the workshop. He went to a rack holding three round steel tanks, each about a foot and a half across. He pulled them from the rack and found a flat box wedged underneath. Luke took it back to the dining room.

"That was the answer. This was under the spherical tanks of nitrogen gas used with the Astronaut Propulsion Unit," said Luke. He held the box up to the camera for the Team to see. Opening it, he found a dozen small audio cassette tapes and a printed playlist. "Cool! I hope they picked out decent music. Althea honey, can I ask you to thank the Three Wise Guys for me, for all the gifts?"

"Of course sweetheart," she said, "Play something good for me when we talk tonight."

"Shall do, darlin'. Thank you for your help, Team. Over and out," said Luke. He closed the connection and went back to work.

#

July 8, 1975

FBI Special Agents Susan Roley and Joanne Pierce met in Roley's tiny, windowless Omaha office to review the Math Bomber case. The ex-marine and ex-nun finished their glazed donut breakfast.

"OK, so now he's planning to target aerospace companies, according to his new Manifesto," Roley said as she rubbed her eyes. Neither Agent had been getting much sleep.

"The Post Office is segregating and inspecting any mail to all the big-name aerospace companies. And each of those companies has told us that, as backup, they will have their mail inspected by bomb-trained security. Hopefully we'll be able to get a hold of some unexploded bombs and get some clues."

"The new Manifesto is an even weirder rant than the first one," Pierce said, sipping her black coffee, "Going on about protecting the Universe from the evil that is humanity."

"I don't think we're going to get very far trying to get into his head. Where do we stand on our long-shot lead from Harry Remains?" asked Roley.

#

Pat Hyland, VP at Hughes Aircraft, kissed his wife Muriel goodbye as he headed out the door to go to work. "Our great-grandkids will be visiting for your birthday party tonight," she said, "If you retired, we could spend more time with them."

"I'm only 75," he said with a smile, "I'll retire when it stops being fun. See you all tonight."

Mail was delivered to the house that afternoon. Among the birthday cards was a small heavy box wrapped in plain brown paper and marked 'Happy Birthday Pat!" Muriel set it on the entryway sideboard with the cards and other presents. At 5:20, Pat called. "Honey, I know I'm usually home by 5:30 and please don't be mad but I just got out of a meeting that ran late. I'll be home as soon as I can."

Muriel sighed. "Pat, the kids will be here any minute. Please don't disappoint them."

"I'll try. I promise," Pat said.

"OK, we won't open any presents till you get here. Not even the mystery present," Muriel laughed.

"OK sweetie, see you soon." Pat hung up. The doorbell rang. Muriel opened the door to see her daughter Ginger and her grandkids. Muriel knelt to hug the kids. The phone rang.

Muriel sighed as she stood up, knee popping, and said, "No rest for the wicked! Come on in while I get that." It was Pat again.

"Honey, what mystery present?" he said.

"What?" she said. The kids were being noisy. She covered her other ear.

"What mystery present?" Pat said, louder. He sounded tense. Muriel was confused.

"I don't know. It's just a box wrapped in brown paper. I didn't see a return address…"

"Muriel!" Pat said, "Don't touch it! Get out of the house right now. Grab the kids and get out! Go down to the Jacobs house. No questions! Just go, please, go right now."

"But…'

"Go, for God's sake!"

The kids could hear Pat's shouts and were staring at her. She laid the phone down. "Kids, a surprise game. Whoever can run down to the corner first gets $5." The kids bolted out the door. Muriel grabbed her daughter's arm and shoved her out the front door after the kids. "Run, Ginger!"

At 72, Muriel wasn't as fast as her daughter. She had just reached the sidewalk when the bomb went off.

Chapter 29: The Hunger Games

July 20, 1975

Luke carefully prepared a dinner. He took six hardcooked eggs and some veggies from the fridge, climbed into the centrifuge, and sat behind the little counter space he had improvised. The centrifugal force of the spinning wheel kept ingredients from floating away. He peeled the eggs, sliced them, and scooped the yolks into a bowl. *Nice and spicy*, he thought, as he added some Tabasco sauce and other spices to the deviled egg mix. Then he made a salad with carrots, radishes, and lettuce he had harvested. He sealed the food in a container along with a bottle of home-made salad dressing for later consumption.

#

Luke loaded the payload into the electrodynamic tether mechanism. Then he put on his spacesuit and checked its life support. It was easy to move the tether assembly in zero gravity though it massed close to a hundred pounds. Still, he was careful as he guided it into the airlock and squeezed himself in with it.

"Control, Skylab 5 here. Preparing to exit air lock with tether assembly," said Luke.

"We copy Luke. You have thirty minutes until scheduled launch of the experiment," said Deke.

Luke opened the airlock to the vacuum of space, reached out, and clipped his personal safety tether to the outside of the station and another short one between his suit and the experiment package. He pushed the electrodynamic tether project out into open space and followed it., clamping his boots to the outside skin of Skylab. Once he felt secure, he
carefully unfolded the solar panels on the tether experiment and verified they were generating power. The view of Earth was beautiful but he couldn't spare the time to take it in. He slowly unrolled the coil of tether from within the package. The tether was a three hundred foot long Kevlar rope with a copper wire running

the length of it and an electron emitter at the far end. When powered up, electrons would flow from the solar panels down the wire and shoot out into space. The uncoiling tether started drifting randomly and looked like it might become a snarled mess. Luke slowly rewound the cable and started over.

"Skylab 5, fifteen minutes to launch," said Deke in his headphones.

"Roger Control."

Luke pushed the weighted end of the cable gently away from the station, toward the bright blue Earth. He tried to feed the cable out at the same speed the end was moving so it wouldn't tangle or bounce back toward him. As the end of the tether moved closer to the Earth, the pull of gravity on it got ever so slightly stronger. So the tether end 'wanted' to move at a faster orbital speed than the station and tugged gently on the rope. The difference was tiny but it was enough to pull the cable straight. Luke finished unrolling the tether.

"Control, tether deployed. I am checking the circuit," Luke said.

Hans came on. "Skylab 5, Hans here. I am receiving a signal from Tether 1 confirming it is functioning. Over."

"Great, Hans. I will release the Tether 1 package on your mark," said Luke.

Silence. *Damn it Hans*, thought Luke. "Over," he said. He felt guilty at his own annoyance. *We're all tense right now.*

"Release at one. 5, 4, 3, …".

Luke unclipped the tether package from Skylab.

"…2, 1, release. Over."

Luke gently pushed the tether package away from him. He knew electrons were now running down the tether, spraying out the end, and joining with the positive ions at the very top of the Earth's atmosphere. That atmosphere was barely detectable 270 miles above the Earth. So even though Skylab was barreling along through those faint traces of air
at 17,000 miles an hour, years would pass before the atmospheric drag slowed Skylab enough to crash it back to Earth.

Luke watched Tether 1 receding into the distance. The electric current running through the cable made a magnetic field that pushed against the magnetic field of the Earth, like the rotor inside an electric motor pushed against the magnetic field in the stator. That push slowed Tether 1 down so it fell into a lower orbit. *All without using any rocket fuel. Cool*, thought Luke.

"Tether 1 launched. Over," he reported. He gazed at the Earth for a while. Clouds and continents rolled past. *So beautiful.* He roused himself. *Back to work.* He got back into the airlock and then the station. Pulling off his spacesuit and clipping it to the wall, he reported in. "Control, back in Skylab safe and sound. How goes Tether 1? Over."

"Hans here. Tether 1 slowing as expected. When we try reversing the electric current, it speeds up and rises in orbit. Very responsive. Just beautiful. On schedule to reach the Soviet's Salyut 4 station in twenty hours."

Luke smiled but did not respond.

"Over," said Hans, laughing.

"Congratulation, Hans. Stay in touch. Over," said Luke.

#

The next day, Commander Pyotyr Klimuk floated outside the Salyut 4 space station, his home for the last month. While he waited, he enjoyed the view of the Earth rolling by.

"NASA Control here. Commander Klimuk, do you copy? Over."

Pyotyr answered in English. "Yes, Control, I read you load and clear. Your mystery package is not yet in view. Over."

"Another ten minutes or so, Commander. Over."

He waited patiently. He had no great expectations for this joint Soviet-US political stunt. *One does what one must.* Soon he saw a flashing light in the distance. "Package in sight, Control."

In minutes he watched the US gadget pass slowly a hundred meters away. "Too far away, Control. Unable to retrieve. Over." He prepared to return to the airlock.

"Commander, we would like to attempt another approach in one orbit. Can you wait ninety minutes? Over."

Pyotyr sighed. He knew his superiors were listening to the exchange. "Of course Control. In the spirit of cooperation between our two great nations, it will not be a problem. Over."

He spent the time sight-seeing. He never grew tired of the changing views of Earth. Seeing lightning strikes and northern lights from above was awesome. The time passed quickly.

"Control here, Commander. Tether 1 should be approaching again. Over."

He saw the blinking light in the distance, growing brighter but barely moving from his point of view as it came almost directly toward him. He readied his spear gun/harpoon, making sure it was tied securely to the station. He knew he had one shot. The American gadget moved slowly past the Soyuz station, perhaps twenty meters away. He fired, aiming not at the package itself but at the tether hanging below it. The cable trailing his harpoon shot past, seemingly missing. But the American's tether moved into his, as he planned. The two tangled and the spear gun was yanked from his hands but stayed tied to the Salyut station. The package swung around. Forgetting his audience, he swore vigorously, fearing a collision. He shouted, "Control, shut off power to the tether now!"

"Power off, over," said Hans.

Thankfully, the package was far enough below him that the gravity gradient kept the now-joined tethers somewhat taut and left the package swinging very slowly like a pendulum. He carefully pulled it closer, winding the tethers around stanchions on the outside of the Soyuz station. Soon he had the experiment in his gloved hands. "Tether 1 has been retrieved Control," he reported. He could hear the Americans cheering in the background. Strapping the gadget to the outside of the Soyuz, as it had served its purpose, he removed the spherical canister payload from the machine, and carried it into the Soyuz.

#

Pyotyr and his fellow cosmonaut Vitali floated near the station's table with the payload canister between them. They smiled for the camera. They knew the American astronaut was linked in to the conversation, along with NASA and their superiors at the Soviet space agency. "We send greetings to NASA and to Lieutenant Priss, our fellow space traveler, as well as thanks for the surprise gift delivered using your wonderful innovation. We hope the electrodynamic tether will help connect future space missions from all countries," said Pyotyr. Expecting some dumb American souvenirs, *probably NASA baseball caps*, he awkwardly unlatched the spherical canister and swung open the lid. His and Vitali's eyes widened with wonder. Eggs and a fresh beautiful green salad lay before them. They were momentarily speechless. They had become resigned to the bland, processed space food provided them. This glorious and generous meal reminded them of what they missed from home. Pyotyr's eyes misted up. Tears pooled annoyingly in zero gravity. He wiped his face on his sleeve. "Lieutenant… spasibo, comrade. Spasibo."

Luke carefully replied, "Niche-e-wa, Commander. It is nothing. Please enjoy."

Chapter 30: Childhood's End

"Pat, can I get you to change your mind?" said Howard.

Pat Hyland, on the other end of the phone call, sounded weak and weary. He had always been a vital and energetic man but now sounded older than his 75 years.

"No, Howard. Muriel is out of the hospital but will be a while recovering. I want to spend every minute I have left with her. It's time I retired. If that damned bomber wanted me out of the picture, well, he succeeded, He wins. Hughes Aerospace will have to find another head of Research and Development. The projects may be slowed a bit but we, you have a great team there. You'll be OK. Goodbye Howard." Pat hung up.

Howard sat alone in the darkened hotel room. He didn't feel 'OK'. He felt like he was in a wagon rolling down a hill, toward an abyss. No way to steer. No brakes. He felt the anxiety building. *Althea, help me.*

#

Years earlier, two small asteroids collided out by Jupiter. Millions of bits of debris flew in all directions, some moving faster and going to higher orbits, some slowing and falling towards the Sun. Months later one tiny chunk of iron passed the orbit of Mars. The Sun's pull on it was gentle but constant. By then it was moving at 20,000 miles per hour. And accelerating.

#

July 26, 1975

Luke was having a teleconference with the cosmonauts.

"Pyotyr, may you and Vitali have a safe journey home today," said Luke.

"Thank you Luke. May you also, when you return to Earth next month. Please come visit us and we will take you to the best bars and restaurants in Moscow."

"I definitely will Pyotyr. And thanks for untangling the electrodynamic tether and sending the unit back to me. Now we can test it further," said Luke.

"It was the least we could do. It was too large anyway for us to claim salvage rights and carry it home, but we did take the opportunity to closely examine its design," said Pyotyr.

Luke laughed. "I would expect nothing less."

#

That night, Althea called Luke. "Hey darlin'," he said. She could hear the Supremes' 'Someday We'll Be Together' playing in the background.

"Hey flyboy. Still missing me?"

"The music gave it away, didn't it?" he said, "Yes, baby, more every day. One month to go."

Althea said, "I miss you too, honey. You know, I went to high school with her."

"Her who?"

"Diana Ross, ya lug. She was in my geometry class at Cass Tech High School. She was good at math and would tutor other kids," Althea said.

"Were you one of them?"

Althea did her best Star Trek impression, "Damn it, Jim, I'm a doctor, not a mathematician!" They laughed.

She said, "You OK, with the Russians leaving orbit and all?"

Luke was a little surprised that she picked up on that. But she knew him better than he knew himself,

"Yeah. It's funny. I didn't physically meet them. Their station's orbit is a hundred miles away from Skylab's. But still, it's a little lonely being the only human in space right now."

"I wish I could be up there with you."

"Me too, darlin'. Maybe someday."

"Speaking of lonely," she said, "Howard is having a crisis. His aide called me. She's having a hard time pulling him out of an emotional tailspin. I think I need to go see him. So I won't be calling you for a day or two. Is that OK?"

"Sure honey. Hope you can help him out."

#

Howard hung up the phone. Althea was coming! That news alone helped calm him. He had made some decisions. Now he had to get some things done before she arrived. He called in his aide.

"Maria, I need a film crew set up in the conference room immediately. I want to make a film record of something." Two hours later Howard stood before the camera. The only people he would allow in the room were the cameraman and sound engineer. Maria had shaved him, trimmed his hair and helped him dress in a suit and tie. He almost felt like he was back in a studio in Hollywood, when he owned RKO Studios.

"Boys, this should be quick, hopefully just one take," Howard said, as he clutched a yellow legal pad, "But give me a moment first." He closed his eyes, took a deep breath and slowly released it, slowing his heart and reducing his anxiety. He wanted to come across to the camera as an executive in complete control of himself. "OK, let's go." When cued, he read aloud from the pad.

Ten minutes later, "Got it Mr. Hughes. I think we're good," said the cameraman. The sound engineer agreed.

"Great," said Hughes. He waved the notepad at them. "Now I need you boys to sign and date this." He set it on the table and stepped back to watch them sign.

"I want that film developed today and the negative and three prints delivered to me ASAP. Send my aide in here on your way out, alright? Thanks."

#

The next day Althea entered Howard's suite. She saw him sitting on the balcony looking out over the ocean. His hearing loss had gotten worse so she called to him loudly so as to not startle him by just walking up.

"Althea! Come join me." He waved at a wicker chair next to his.

"Howard, how are you doing? Maria was concerned that you were …."

"Having an 'episode'?" he asked.

"Yes."

"Well, I guess I was feeling pretty intense anxiety, yeah. I mean, weeks ago my former aide was killed when he opened a bomb mailed to me. Then Pat Hyland's wife gets a concussion and a broken arm from another bomb. So Pat resigned. The FBI seems helpless against this god-damned Math Bomber. So, yes, I was upset."

"And yet here you sit, looking relaxed and almost cheerful," Althea said.

"Having you here…".

"Thank you but bullshit, Howard. You've got something going on."

Howard grinned. "Direct as always, Doc. That's one reason I love you." He took two flat boxes from the table between them and handed them to Althea. "I'd like you to mail that one to Harry when you get back to the States. The other is for you. I have a third one in my safe here."

"What are they?"

"My Last Will and Testament. I made Harry my Executor. He gets the original paper Will, you and I get photocopies. I'd send a set to Luke but he's a little hard to reach right now. All the copies include a reel of film of me reading it aloud, so no one can claim it's a forgery later when, you know…".

"Howard! Is there something you want to tell me? The results of your last physical were good, considering…". She paused, embarrassed.

"Considering what terrible shape I'm in?" said Howard smiling, "Doc, we both know I have a lot of damage from my plane crash thirty years ago and then all the drugs for years after that. I can't keep pretending I'm going to live forever. Talking to Pat Hyland made me think about what little time I have left. Too little to finish our big projects, anyway. You and Harry and Luke will have to carry on creating that space-faring civilization."

Althea looked like she was going to cry.

"Geez, Doc, what kind of bedside manner is that?" Howard smiled. "We're all going to die. Accepting that has given me some peace and clarity. When my little red wagon, with me in it, flies off the edge of the cliff into the Great Beyond, I want to have my hands in the air, yelling 'Wheee!'".

Then he looked serious. "I'm tired of being afraid, Doc."

Althea knew he wouldn't want to be hugged. Taking his hand might be OK. It was.

#

Luke had just gone to bed when the tiny lump of iron passed the Moon, now moving at 30,000 miles per hour.

#

Luke settled into the routine of collecting samples and data, caring for the plants and animals, and maintaining the station. The rabbits were giving birth to litters of kits. Some were stillborn or malformed and died in days.. Rachel had told him that rabbits had a high infant mortality rate even on Earth. But it seemed pretty clear that in lower gravity it was even harder to gestate healthy offspring. Luke froze the sad little bodies to return to Earth for analysis. He left the survivors in the care of their mothers.

As for the chickens, Gregory Peck, the matriarch, had established her pecking order and no longer crowed at random moments, thank God. Many of the fertilized eggs produced damaged chicks or never hatched. Luke put the few healthy ones in their own cage.

In his free time, Luke read from the collection of science fiction magazines and novels that Harry had given him as a going-away present. Not on paper but in the form of microfiche, 4 by 5 sheets of film, with a hundred pages shrunk to fit on each sheet. Luke used a hand-held gadget with a backlit lense to magnify the images. While eating breakfast at the food tray pedestal, feet hooked over the seat's base, Luke was re-reading 'Caves of Steel' by Isaac Asimov, one of his favorites.

#

If there had been no Skylab 5 mission and so no capsule docked to the station, the tiny meteor would have missed the station and ended its journey burning up in the atmosphere, making a pretty shooting star. Instead, the little lump of iron, small as a nickel but traveling at 35,000 miles per hour, hit the Command Module with the energy of a hand grenade. It smashed into a hydrazine fuel tank. Shrapnel blasted the control panel and punched holes in the walls of the capsule.

#

The shock reverberated through the station. The chickens fluttered in their cages and the rabbits squealed. Luke jumped to turn off the fans in the ventilating system. Other than the chickens 'awking' softly, the station was quiet now. Luke checked the station air pressure. No change. Good. He listened for the 'hiss' of a leak. Nothing.

Luke called in.

"Control, apparently the station has just been hit by something. I've turned off the fans and don't hear any obvious leaks. Can you run through all systems for me?"

Deke was in Control and responded, "Shall do, Luke. Keep checking for leaks. Be sure all hatches are sealed."

"Hatches already sealed. Will keep checking."

Luke found a waste bag of feathers dropped by the chickens that he had collected doing cleanup. He released a few handfuls of down and let it drift through the station. It would be a hassle to clean up later but might show air flowing toward any punctures. He grabbed a repair kit that included adhesive patches and flew up and down the length of the station, watching the feathers and listening for leaks. Nothing. Whatever Deke found out in a systems review, Luke knew he would have to inspect the exterior of the station. So he didn't wait for orders but started suiting up. He was near the airlock adaptor when Deke called.

"We're getting weird data from the Command Service Module. Hard to decipher. All other systems normal."

"OK," said Luke, "I'm entering the airlock and will inspect

the CSM."

He closed his helmet, checked the suit's systems, and entered the airlock passage. He closed the hatch to the Workshop behind him. Checking a gage on the wall Luke said, "Looks like zero air pressure within the CSM. I'm going to try entering it."

He spilled air from the airlock and felt his suit swell up. Opening the hatch to the capsule, Luke saw shafts of sunlight streaming through the space within. Shards of metal and fiberglass formed a sparkling cloud in the capsule. Debris drifted out into space through jagged holes in the capsule walls.

"Well, *that* doesn't look good."

Luke described the situation to Deke who replied "Shit."

"Shit indeed," said Luke. He wondered for a moment if he could salvage any supplies from within the capsule but decided it was too dangerous; he might tear his suit. He carefully brushed away some debris that had floated onto the edge of the hatch opening and closed it. He moved to an airlock door leading to the exterior of the station.

"I've sealed the hatch to the CSM. I'm now entering the EVA airlock to check outside."

Luke moved slower than usual, inspecting every surface for damage as he entered open space. The walls of the Command Module were riddled with holes. Luke circled the capsule, taking photos. The edges of the largest hole he found were bent inwards.

"Something definitely punched through from outside. It wasn't an explosion from within, at least initially."

Luke moved around the outside of the station. The Telescope Mount, with its four wings of solar panels, seemed unharmed. He could see a few dents in the skin of the Multiple Docking Adaptor but no holes or escaping air.

"Control, damage seems pretty confined to the CSM. So, other than having no ride home, everything's peachy."

#

Deke and The Team were teleconferencing with Luke. He was back at the station's kitchen table. Deke thought he looked grim but calm, with his hands clasped together. Deke glanced at Althea. The same expression and posture, almost as if it was her way to be with Luke. Billie sat to one side of her, Rachel on the other, obviously for moral support. *OK, let's get on with this*, Deke thought.

"Luke, bottom line: you are safe but stuck. Temporarily. We have started prepping a launch to retrieve you ASAP," Deke said.

"ASAP? The mission has thirty days to go," said Luke.

Althea sat straighter. "Luke! Be reasonable! The mission is compromised. It's not safe…"

"Why not? The CSM was the only thing damaged. I have supplies for another month, at least."

Deke held up a hand. Althea and Luke shut up but the tension between them was high.

"Althea, I'm sorry I wasn't more clear but it's going to take twenty-eight days to prep the Saturn B1 and launch pad anyway," Deke said. She glared at him.

"Why? What if there was some medical emergency and he had to be retrieved immediately? Couldn't you keep the rocket prepped and ready to launch?"

Deke was about to answer but Luke interrupted.

"Darlin', no, it just doesn't work that way…"

"Don't 'darlin' me!" Althea looked like she was about to explode.

"Doctor?," said a voice quietly. It was Peter. Everyone looked at him in surprise.

Althea stared at him, her chin quivering.

"We'll take care of him. We always have and always will," Peter said.

Althea put her face in her hands.

#

Squealing bearings woke Luke from a fitful sleep. *Another motor failing on the centrifuge.* He blearily rubbed his eyes and, moving slowly so the centrifuge could adjust more easily to his shifting weight, sat up and climbed out into the workshop. He unpacked a spare motor. *Christ, only one left after this.* Luke removed the bad motor and bolted in the spare. He checked the time. *OK, day shift has started in Control.* He called down and asked for a private teleconference with Peter.

"Peter, what the hell? Another motor failed on the centrifuge and I'm down to one spare. Where did you buy these damn things, North Korea?" Luke said. He felt like his world was falling apart. Skylab seemed cursed. Solar panels and sunshield ripped off when it was first launched. The first crew managed to jury-rig a reflective umbrella to control the heat and worked around the reduced power. Those men at least had each other for support. Althea was taking a break from work. No calls from her for three days. Luke was alone and he felt it.

"Sorry Luke. We dug into the paperwork from the vendor and we suspect they skipped testing the motors and faked the data," said Peter. "I know that doesn't help you but..".

"No, it doesn't," said Luke, He rubbed his face in irritation. "Well, if the centrifuge breaks down, we'll just have a smaller data set on the effects of variable gravity. OK, bye Peter."

"No wait, Luke!" Peter said. He looked uncomfortable.

"What is it?" asked Luke.

"It's about Althea, I mean Dr. Nespla."

"'Althea' is OK, Peter. What's up? How is she?"

"Rachel and Billy are spending a lot of time with her. I guess they're helping her feel better. They thought I should be the one to talk to you, I think maybe since we're both mechanical engineers? I don't know" said Peter.

Luke was actually feeling better as he felt sympathy for the poor little guy. Peter was not strong on human interactions. "So do you have some thoughts on Althea and me?" asked Luke.

"Yes". Then silence.

"And they are…?"

"I think she is torn up that she can't help you. You and I like having physical problems to solve," Peter said, "Althea likes helping people, saving people. Maybe that's why she became a doctor? Anyway, I wonder if she should be off the Team."

Luke was surprised. "Really?"

"She's a doctor, not a scientist," said Peter. Luke smiled. *He forgot to say 'Dammit Jim'.*

Peter continued, "If she goes back to the hospital on Grand Bahama Island, then she could be doing what she does best. Maybe that would make her happier. She loves you but she's stressed out. I would miss her though," said Peter.

"Me too," said Luke. *I miss her now.* "Peter, have you mentioned this to Althea, Rachel, or Billie?"

"No."

"Then please do sit down with all of them and talk about it. If Althea needs that, I want her to do it," said Luke.

"OK, I will. Bye Luke. I mean, 'Over'," said Peter. He hung up.

Luke floated quietly for a minute. *25 days and counting.*

Chapter 31: The World Set Free

It was late afternoon when the two FBI agents got out of their rental car and walked to the manager's office at the Dew Drop Inn motel. "Number fifty-two on our list," said Joanne Pierce, checking her clipboard.

"Whatever," said Susan Roley wearily, "Maybe this one will actually remember a customer from a year ago." She was starting to think they were on a wild goose chase, that Harry Remain's theory that Ted had escaped from prison and became the Math Bomber was bogus. Harry had helped put Ted in prison. Maybe Harry felt guilty about his own father dying in a bomb blast for some reason and his Ted-theory supported that guilt in some weird way. Susan rubbed her eyes tiredly. Whatever. If their effort in Michigan fizzled, they would head back to their offices and try to think of something else to try. A Math Bomber task force had been formed and she and Pierce were now simply two of many agents working the case. If they didn't find anything useful soon, they might be reassigned

The manager stood up from his desk behind the counter as they entered. His eyes flicked between the two women. "Good afternoon. Would you be wanting one room or two?"

Pierce just smiled sweetly. Roley flashed her FBI badge and glanced at the nameplate on his desk. "Neither actually, Mr. Jackson. I'm FBI Special Agent Roley and this is Special Agent Pierce. We're trying to get some information that may help us find an escaped prisoner."

Jackson frowned. "Women FBI agents? Is that a thing?"

They had been getting this reaction a lot. Roley was tired of it and about to set him straight when

Pierce leaned in over the counter. "Yes, Andy, pretty wild isn't it? We're the first two. If you could help us, we would.. I would.. really appreciate it. I'm Joanne."

Roley thought, *Well, at least she's not batting her eyes at him. Guess I'm playing Bad Cop this time.*

The manager's expression softened. "Nice to meet you Joanne."

"Mr. Jackson," said Roley bruskly, "We're wondering if, about a year ago, you may have rented a room to this fellow." She opened a folder and pulled out a Polaroid of her boss glowering into the camera. Andy examined it. "No, can't say I remember him."

"How about this one?" She handed him a photo of Roy Scheider, the actor from the current blockbuster movie *Jaws*. Andy blinked in puzzlement, "Isn't he in that shark movie?"

Joanne took the photo from him and glanced at it, "I think you're right. How about this guy?" She showed him a photo of Ted.

Roley saw a flash of recognition in Andy's eyes and then his posture, his expression all radiated 'Caution'. "Hmm, I'm not sure. I don't think so," said Andy.

Bingo, thought Roley. "Mr. Jackson, we believe this man may have killed eleven people since he escaped from prison. Anyone aiding him in his escape could be considered an accomplice to murder."

Jackson's eyes widened in alarm.

"On the other hand," said Pierce, "Anyone providing information leading to his capture could share in any reward."

"There's a reward?" said Jackson.

"The size of the reward is being discussed," said Pierce.

First I've heard of it, thought Roley.

"If we keep collecting information from people, obviously any such reward would be split up among more people. So, the sooner he's captured…" she finished, smiling.

"Well, now that I think about it, he does look familiar."

"Great!" said Pierce, "Can we see your guest books from late 1973? That could be really helpful."

Jackson opened the bottom drawer of his desk and started rummaging through it. Roley saw a stack of Playboy magazines on top. Jackson rolled his swivel chair around the drawer, obviously and awkwardly trying to hide them from the two women. Roley glanced at Pierce who made a mock expression of shock.

Jackson pulled a wide green book from the drawer, opened it and checked the dates on the first and last pages. He set it aside and checked another one. "Yeah, here we go," He lay it on the counter.

Roley opened it and flipped pages until she found entries around the date of the prison explosion. There were three names on the exact date. She turned the book around to face Jackson and pointed at the entries. "Do any of these names bring anyone to mind?"

Jackson leaned over to read the entries. Pierce laid a hand on his arm and said, "Think hard, Andy."

Roley thought, *Jeez, Joanne, lighten up! You'll just distract him.*

Jackson made a show of concentrating, furrowing his brow and bending over to peer at the book.

He knows something, thought Roley.

Jackson seemed to come to a decision. He pointed to one entry. "I think this might be that guy."

Roley turned the book around to face the agents. "Paul Erlich," she read aloud. She looked at Pierce who gave a head-tilt and shrug, obviously not getting the significance.

Roley said, "Paul Erlich is a biologist who wrote *The Population Bomb*, predicting world famines and mass deaths from overpopulation in the '70s. Using his name as an alias is right up Ted's alley."

"Ted?" said Jackson.

"The actual name of our suspect," said Pierce.

Roley saw an odd expression pass over Jackson's face. "Or did you know him by another name, not Paul or Ted?" she asked.

Pierce pointed at the dates of check-in and check-out on the guest book. "It seems he stayed here for almost a month. Did you get to know him at all, Andy?"

Jackson hesitated. Pierce held her hands palms up, as if weighing two choices. "Remember Andy," she tilted one hand toward Roley, "Accomplice". She lay the other hand on his arm. "Or reward."

"OK, OK. We didn't talk much but I do remember that he asked for a favor that was kinda weird. He said he needed to apply for a Social Security number, which I thought was strange, I mean, he was in his thirties so how could he not have one? Anyway, he gave me a long story about his parents being missionaries overseas, whatever. He asked me to sign a letter saying he worked for me. I couldn't see the harm in that so…," Jackson paused, obviously wondering if he had just confessed to a Federal crime.

"That's cool, Andy. Not a problem. What happened then?" asked Pierce.

"Well, in a few weeks he got mail from the government. I remember because we almost never get mail for guests. Then he checked out."

Roley said, "So, Mr. Jackson, the name he used on the letter to Social Security. It wasn't Ted or Paul, was it?"

"No. I remember thinking when I signed the letter that it was odd that the name he gave was different from Paul."

The two women looked at him expectantly.

"But, sorry, I don't remember what it was, just that it was different. I mean, that was more than a year ago."

Roley sighed.

Pierce asked, "Andy, do you recall what kind of vehicle he drove?"

"It was a pickup truck, gray I think."

"OK Mr. Jackson," said Roley, "We'll need to take this guestbook with us as evidence. It will eventually be returned to you. Thank you for your cooperation."

Pierce handed Jackson her card. "Andy, if you remember anything else about that guest, anything at all, please let us know ASAP. We're very grateful for your assistance."

"Sure Joanne, glad to help," said Jackson.

The agents sat in their car outside the motel. Roley was frustrated. "So close!"

Pierce said, "No, it's good. We have a positive ID from a witness. Social Security didn't cooperate when we asked for a list of all applicants around the time of the explosion because they said it was 'too broad, an invasion of privacy, a fishing expedition'. Now we have the address where Ted's new Social Security card was sent and a more precise date for when it was issued."

Roley sighed. "You're right. I'm just tired. Tomorrow morning we'll call them and try again."

Pierce was rummaging through a file. She pulled out a paper. "Hey, remember Corbin, the guy who visited the prison the night of the explosion? Here's the statement of the prison guard who waved Corbin's pickup truck through the gate." She scanned the sheet.

"A gray pickup truck". She grinned triumphantly at Roley.

#

It was Althea's decision to leave The Team but she felt like she was being fired as she packed personal items from her desk into a small cardboard box. An official NASA photo of Luke proudly wearing his spacesuit. A seashell from a beach walk on their honeymoon. Another photo, this one of the entire Team looking all eager and united, ready to create the future. She peered at her own smiling face in the photo. What had changed? Now she felt sad and anxious. She watched the other Team members working at their desks. There wasn't really much for her to do here anyway. NASA doctors would keep collecting data on Luke's well-being. Her packed suitcase was in the trunk of Luke's red and white Thunderbird. Soon she'd be driving it to the airport to leave for Grand Bahama Island. Then she could be like other astronaut wives, sitting at home worrying and feeling useless instead of watching Luke be in danger live from Ground Control and feeling useless. NASA would patch her phone calls from there up to Skylab every night. She felt guilty. She had neglected Luke for days, just because she felt overwhelmed with anxiety about his safety.

Althea carried the box to another desk. "Peter, can I ask you to take this stuff back to my apartment? The manager will know to let you in. I'll be catching a plane to Grand Bahama Island in a couple of hours so I'm going to drive straight to the airport from here."

"Sure Althea. I'll water your houseplants too, until you and Luke return."

Althea nodded sadly. For the last year Luke and The Team had been totally focused on the Skylab 5 mission. She wasn't sure what came next in their lives. Everything felt like it was stuck or falling apart. Howard's health was in a sharp decline, one reason she was headed back to the island. Harry was immersed in running hotels and casinos and had no time for SF conventions or, apparently, just having fun. It seemed like his father's death had kicked the heart out of him. Luke was stuck in a ramshackle space station that seemed held together with paper clips and duct tape. The dream of a space-faring civilization felt pretty silly and hollow.

Peter saw the sadness on Althea's face and groped for a way to cheer her up or, at least, distract her. "Say Doc, before you go, can you help me with a little chore?"

"Sure Peter. What is it?"

"I've got to do a bit of inventory and organizing of stuff in storage. Can I ask you to record the items on a list as I move things around?"

"I really need to leave in an hour or so…"

"It should go pretty quick with the two of us doing it. Here," he said as he handed her a headset, "You can sit here with the clipboard and I'll talk to you from the storage area. It'll be fun, like we're on a mission!"

"Right," she said. *Just how I want to spend my last day on The Team.* But Peter was a sweet little guy so she humored him.

#

Almost an hour had passed as Peter moved and meticulously described each item for Althea to record. He was starting to worry that Althea might be getting bored.

Peter said, "Almost done, Doc. Now at the SES. Over."

"SES?," said Althea.

"Student Experiment Shelf," he replied, "Now relocating duplicate experiments to create greater volume for supplies. Over."

Picking up a green plastic cube, Peter said, "Item #27, cube, plastic, green, approximately six inches on a side." There was a loud 'click' from within the cube. Startled, Peter dropped it. "Oops."

The cube exploded.

#

Althea heard the blast and ripped off her headphones,. She ran down the hall and found Peter in the doorway of the storage room, laying in a pool of blood, his legs mangled and pulsing more blood. Two NASA engineers were standing gaping at the scene. Althea snapped at them, "Give me your neckties! Now!"

They looked confused but obeyed. She used the ties to make tourniquets above Peter's knees. He was unconscious and pale as a sheet of paper. Althea couldn't do more for him at the moment so she ran to an office and grabbed a phone. She called for an ambulance and directed them to the scene. Running back into the hallway, she pointed to the two engineers who were still gaping at Peter. "You two!"

They pulled their eyes from the carnage and stared at her, wide-eyed.

"Go out that exit door."

Pointing at one of them, "You! Hold the door open, do not let it close. You!," pointing at the other man, "Go outside and wave down the ambulance, direct them here to Peter. Move it!"

They nodded and moved. Althea found their suit coats in an office and lay them over Peter for warmth. She knelt next to him with her hand on his shoulder and waited.

#

The emergency crew was loading Peter into the ambulance. Althea was about to get in as well when Rachel ran up.

"Althea, you need to see Deke in The Team office. I'll ride with Peter.".

Althea saw the stress in Rachel's face and asked no questions. She just nodded and headed back to her desk. She stopped at a restroom to wash Peter's blood from her hands. She couldn't do anything about the spatters on her clothes.

As she walked into the office, the rest of the Team converged on her with questions. Some looked horrified at the blood on her clothes. Deke came in and pulled a chair up to her desk. Peter's chair, she noticed irrelevantly. Deke held his hands up to hush the group.

"Althea, Rachel's gone with Peter to the hospital…".

She nodded.

"..and she'll keep us all informed on his status. Security is at the scene of the explosion. They've called in the local bomb squad and the FBI. I'm sure they'll have some questions for you. That's why I asked Rachel to stay with Peter instead of you. Everybody's speculating that the device was planted in the storeroom somehow by the Math Bomber. You were talking to Peter when it happened, right?" Deke asked.

"Yes, we had an audio link. He was going through the stuff on the shelves of the storeroom when it happened," Althea said.

Her eyes widened.

"The student experiments. Peter was moving the duplicate student experiments. Copies of the ones onboard Skylab. With Luke."

#

Luke was on his sleeping pad in the centrifuge, reading the Gore Vidal article in Playboy. He heard a loud 'click'.

Chapter 32: The Cold Equations

The 'click' seemed to have come from a spot on the centrifuge opposite his sleeping pad. Luke stored items there that he didn't use often or at all, like some of the student experiments that didn't require any attention. He used the mass of all the items to counter his own mass, keeping the centrifuge balanced and reducing load on the motors. He started moving around the centrifuge to investigate.

"Luke! Stop whatever you're doing! Don't move!" Deke's voice rang out from Control.

Luke froze. "OK, understood. What's up?"

"A bomb exploded here in the Operations Building. We think it may have been set by the Math Bomber."

"Althea! Is Althea OK?"

She answered, "Yes Luke, I'm fine but I'm afraid Peter is in critical condition."

"Peter? That's awful!" said Luke, "But why the order for me to freeze? I don't understand."

Deke said, "We're investigating but we think the bomb may have been one of the duplicate student science experiments. So don't touch anything while we figure this out."

"But those were submitted by high school students… oh right, by their science teachers. What the hell, the Math Bomber is a science teacher?" said Luke. "Wouldn't bombing NASA that way lead to kind of a short list of suspects? I got the impression he was smarter than that."

Althea said. "Luke, if the Math Bomber did this then he had to make two bombs. He wouldn't know which one would stay at NASA and which would launch with you. The one on the shelf wasn't supposed to go off but did, for some reason. But the one with you…," she finished quietly.

"Darlin', I'm OK, we'll figure this out."

Hans had been sitting quietly listening. Now he said, "Deke, can I ask some questions?"

"Sure."

"Althea, you were talking to Peter via headset when it

happened, right?" Hans said.

"Yes. I was writing down his descriptions as he did inventory."

"Do you remember what he said right before, you know..?"

Althea looked up like some people do when they are trying to recall something. "He said, 'Item #27, cube, plastic, green, approximately six inches on a side'." She paused. "Then I heard a loud 'click' and Peter said 'Oops'."

"Oops?"

"Oops."

"That's all?"

"Yes," said Althea.

"Sounds to me like Peter dropped the cube," said Hans.

"So?" Deke said.

"That means the cube was in free-fall, basically in zero gravity, for…," he paused and did head-math, "half a second before it would have hit the floor. I think the 'click' you and Peter heard, Althea, was a timer in the cube arming the bomb, allowing it to explode if a sensor in it 'thought' the bomb was in zero gravity."

Althea said, "So if Peter hadn't dropped the cube, it would still just be sitting on the shelf?"

"Probably."

Luke said, "I hate to say this but, a second before y'all called me, I heard a click." He heard gasps from the Team.

"Where from?" Hans said. "Could you tell?"

"It was on the centrifuge, opposite my sleeping pad."

"So the bomb in Skylab hasn't gone off because…," said Deke.

Luke answered. "Because it's sitting in the centrifuge with me. It 'thinks' it's feeling gravity so the pressure switch, or whatever, in it is keeping the bomb from exploding."

Althea said, "But the centrifuge is only simulating like 2/3 of Earth's gravity, right? So that switch could be right on the edge of closing?"

The others in the room tried to make comforting comments about Luke being safe but he simply felt proud of Althea. "Thinking like an engineer, darlin'. I knew I would rub off on you."

"Hush. So what do we do Deke?," Althea said. "Can we speed up the launch to go get Luke? We can't let him sit with an armed bomb for twenty-three days. And what the hell is NASA doing, letting a bomb get onboard in the first place? Don't you check those experiments for safety?"

Luke was about to defend NASA and the schedule with some comment like 'I'm sure there were forms submitted with the experiments claiming they were safe. And if we speed up the launch it could endanger that crew.' *But, you know*, he thought, *screw it. This time. I agree with Althea. Let Deke deal with an angry black woman.*

Deke tried, "Doctor, after we get Luke safely back, I will be happy to put the two of you on a Lessons-Learned committee to address that security issue. As for the launch, the schedule was already designed to be as quick as possible without adding undo risk to the rescue crew. Right now, I think we need to focus on how to deal with that bomb."

"I agree," said Althea. Deke looked relieved.

Luke added, "NASA might also help the FBI arrest a certain science teacher."

"Already on it," said Deke. "Team, let's get with the local bomb squad and start figuring out a way to defuse that bomb. Althea, that includes you. You already missed your plane, right?"

"Oh, I'm not going anywhere. This is one astronaut's wife who's going to stay in the room and fight for her man. I'm not anxious now, I'm pissed off."

#

Deke was on the phone with an FBI agent at the Miami office. He had the list of student science experiments in front of him.

Deke said "We think the bomb came from Butte Montana High School at 3225 Wharton Street. W-H-A-R-T-O-N. It was sent to us disguised as a student science experiment. The 'science teacher' who submitted it was …"

#

"Carl Frikes," Susan Roley said to her boss. "Social Security coughed up Ted's new identity and current address. He's in Butte Montana. I request that Agent Pierce and I fly there and assist in his arrest."

Her boss sat behind his desk and looked at her thoughtfully. He was about to say something when his phone rang. He picked it up and listened for a minute.

"Carl Frikes, eh? F-R-I-K-E-S ? Butte, Montana High school? OK thanks." He hung up.

Shit, thought Roley. She slumped in her seat. *The Miami office has beaten me to Ted. Beaten me and Pierce*, she amended guiltily.

"OK, you and Pierce get your butts to Butte."

She sat up, surprised.

"You two found him first, you know he's Ted, they don't. And I'll be damned if I let the Miami office get credit for the arrest. Get going."

"Yes sir!"

#

"OK, I'm going to move the animals out of the centrifuge now," Luke said. Moving slow as a snail, he started unclipping the animal cages from the frame of the centrifuge. He carried each toward the center axis of the centrifuge, moving slowly to give the mechanism time to rebalance smoothly.

"Why bother Luke?" asked Billie. "I don't mean to be insensitive but will they be any safer outside the centrifuge?"

"Billie, I'm sure as hell not going to continue climbing in and out to feed and water them, putting a strain on the mechanism every time. All of us will be living in zero-gee for the rest of the mission. It messes up the gestation experiment but that's life." He gently pushed the cage with Gregory Peck out of the centrifuge and let it float away, Gregory protesting loudly.

Soon the other end of the workshop was full of floating cages, bouncing off each other. Animal waste and feed was trailing the cages like comet tails.

I'm going to need to wear a mask until I figure out their new living arrangements. What a freaking mess.

#

Rachel entered The Team office to see the desks pushed aside and rows of chairs set up in front of the large white board. The group gathered around her. "How's Peter doing?" asked Billie.

"He's off Critical status. The blood loss almost killed him."

"So he'll be OK?" asked Hans.

Rachel stared at him. "He's lost both legs below the knee. So, no, I don't think he'll be OK." Hans blanched and looked grief-stricken. Billie lay a hand on his shoulder.

"But he's alive, Hans." He nodded, tears on his face.

"I'm sorry," said Rachel, "It's been hard sitting in an Emergency waiting room, seeing accident and trauma victims pass through. And then seeing Peter all..." She couldn't finish. She looked at Althea. "I don't know how you deal with it."

Althea shrugged. "You help as best you can. Move on and help again. You forgive yourself for not saving everyone and tell yourself that doing something is better than doing nothing."

Rachel said, "Deke told me what's happening." She grabbed some markers. "My expertise in biology can probably contribute nothing to this process. You guys throw ideas out and I'll record them on the board."

As she spoke, Luke appeared on a monitor. Deke came in and strangers filed in after him. They took seats in the second row and The Team sat in front. Billie sat next to Althea.

Deke said "We'll skip names for now. I'll just say that our visitors include agents from the Miami FBI office..". Two men raised hands. "NASA Security officers...". More hands. "And local Bomb Squad officers." Nods.

Billie said, "Deke, we were about to start brainstorming ideas to help Luke. Why don't we start and consult our guests as we go?"

Deke nodded and waved for her to continue.

Billie projected a slide on the wall. Photos of the student experiments had been taken when they were received at NASA. This one showed a green plastic cube.

"This item and a duplicate were submitted as student experiments to NASA. We believe they were actually bombs. One almost killed our Team member. It was supposed to contain layers of various non-hazardous materials. It would simply sit passively through the mission, being exposed to cosmic rays. When returned to Earth, the students would examine the layers for changes and interactions." She went on to relate Peter's conversation with Althea and The Team's thoughts about the bomb on Skylab.

Hans turned to the bomb squad members. "We're assuming the explosive is C4. Does that seem reasonable?"

Bomb Squad Guy #1 said, "Given the damage to the storage room and the size of the bomb, yes, it most likely was C4."

Hans continued,"Brainstorm plan #1: Freeze the bomb. If Luke could freeze the C4 somehow, could that keep it from exploding?"

Bomb Squad Guy #2 spoke up. "Possibly. When I was in training in the Army, if weather conditions were cold enough, sometimes the blasting cap stuck in the block of C4 would just blow it into chunks
instead of igniting it."

Hans said, "So maybe that's a possibility. We're brainstorming so no critiques until we can't think of any more plans, OK? Next idea?"

After an hour or so they stalled out so Rachel ran through the list of ideas. "Time to critique. Plan #1: Freeze the bomb".

Luke said, "I have a freezer onboard so maybe I could make a lot of ice and pack it around the bomb? Then shove it out an airlock?"

"Packing the ice could jostle the bomb switch. Also, the blasting cap would still go off in your hands when you moved the bomb," said Bomb Squad Guy #2.

Rachel read, "Plan 2: Build a small portable centrifuge, spin up the bomb, carry it to an airlock, and shove it out into space."

BSG #1 said "Just picking it up could set it off."

"Plan 3: Burn it up."

BSG #2 said "It's true C4 will burn. It needs a blasting cap to explode. When I was in Vietnam, we would sometimes use slices of C4 as fuel to cook our rations...."

"Christ," muttered Billie.

"...but the heat could close the circuit in the bomb before the C4 was safely consumed."

Deke added, "Also, a raging chemical fire in a space station? Let's not."

Rachel read, "Plan 4: Capture the Math Bomber and 'ask' him for advice on disarming the bomb."

Althea said, "Do any of us believe he would cooperate? I don't."

"Plan 5: Leave the Workshop where the bomb is, retreat to the Airlock Module, close the hatch between the two, and wait for rescue."

Deke said, "If the bomb went off, it wouldn't matter where you were in the station. The blast might not kill you but the life support would be destroyed."

He glanced at Althea and saw her jaw tighten but she just said, "Keep going Rachel."

"Plan 6: Fix the Command Module capsule and just leave."

Luke said, "It's way too damaged. The walls are like swiss cheese and the hydrazine maneuvering fuel is gone."

Rachel continued. "Plan 7: Patch the capsule, move solar panels from the Telescope Mount to the capsule, attach the electrodynamic tether, board the capsule, use the tether to lower the capsule's orbit until it re-enters the atmosphere."

Luke replied, "Again, the Command Module is just too damaged. Also, re-entry into the atmosphere would be way too uncontrolled. I could end up in the Pacific a thousand miles from any ship. And a tether and solar panels mounted on the capsule would make flight control impossible. So, nope."

Rachel looked apologetic. "Last idea. Plan 8: Ask the Russians for help."

"I've already asked," Deke said, "They can't get a launch ready any faster than we can."

Everyone sat silently. Billie looked around. Like her, no one could face Luke on the monitor, watching them all fail him. Billie looked at Althea. Her eyes were closed and her fingers rested on her knees, tapping furiously. Billie wanted to touch her shoulder sympathetically but thought she might explode.

Althea snapped her fingers. "I've got it…"

Chapter 33: Plan 9 From Outer Space

Ted was eating lunch at his desk when the Principal stuck his head into the classroom.

"Carl! I just heard on the radio that NASA has been hit with a bomb in Florida. Everyone's saying that it's probably the Math Bomber. Thought you'd want to know, since your kids sent that experiment in to NASA. If you talk about the bomb with your students, please keep the discussion calm and tell them the authorities are working hard on catching him. OK?" He left.

Ted sat holding his sandwich halfway to his mouth. *Shit, shit, shit. The wrong bomb went off.* He took a deep breath to calm himself and stood up. He walked to the parking lot, fortunately not bumping into the Principal or other teachers. He drove his old car to the bank and emptied his account, giving the teller a story about a family emergency. Then he drove straight out of town, not wasting time going to his house. He had a bug-out bag in the trunk, full of essentials, in case things fell apart. *Looks like they are*, he thought. He felt panic rising in him and quelled it with anger. *Time to fight a new way. Go further underground. Spread the word.* He had sometimes thought about joining with other revolutionaries but he hated being in a group, making compromises, having to listen to idiots with idiotic ideas. *Best to stay alone.* The thought of returning to prison screamed in his brain and he almost drove through a red light. *No, no, no, can't get pulled over. Concentrate on the plan.* He drove on.

#

Althea said, "Luke, you're a pilot."

Silence all around. Finally, Luke said, "Why, yes I am. Go on."

"So fly Skylab. Fly it to Salyut 4 and move in there. Away from the bomb. And wait for rescue."

More silence. Rachel got up, went to the whiteboard and wrote 'Plan 9: Fly to Salyut 4'.

Deke said, "There's not enough fuel on Skylab for the

attitude engines to do that."

Hans said, "So we use the electrodynamic tether, powered by Skylab's solar panels. Save the attitude engines for course adjustment. I think this could work."

Deke said, "I'll call the Russians and enlist their help, see how much air and other supplies are available in their station. And if they locked the damned door."

Rachel wiped the board clean and started making notes. Luke interrupted the vigorous discussion. "Guys." They quieted. "You all hammer out the details on Althea's plan and get back to me ASAP. I'll throw my two cents in then. Right now, I have to deal with this mess. Darlin', I swear I won't go near the bomb, fuss with it, jiggle it, or make eye contact. OK? I am totally focused on getting home to you. I love you."

"Love you too, flyboy," she said softly. He hung up.

#

Luke jury-rigged a sheet of air filter material over the station's ventilation fan intake duct. Then he snagged each floating critter cage and clipped them over the filter. He hoped the air flowing into the duct would help hold the animal's pee, poop, and spilled food against pads on the floor of each cage. *Though it'll probably make the place stink even more than it does now.* The thought of simply killing the animals passed through his mind. *No.* The variable gravity experiment was pretty much shot now anyway. *No.* Keeping them alive would make Althea's plan harder to do. *No.* He thought of the bomber. *I will not let that bastard win. I came to do science, however badly, and that's just what I'm going to do.*

A motor on the centrifuge started squealing.
Luke put his hands over his eyes and shuddered. A wave of despair passed through him. He imagined Althea with him. He had only cried in front of her once. He did now. His engineer's mind watched. Let the excess pressure vent. Keep it going. *Breathe deep,* he thought. When the tears started feeling a bit forced, he stopped and wiped his eyes. *Now to replace that damned motor.* He dug out the last spare motor and a wrench.

#

Agents Roley and Pierce landed at Bert Mooney Airport in Butte. A dozen people milled around in the lobby. A stranger walked up and smiled broadly. "Joanne! Susan! How was your flight?" He leaned in to give Pierce a hug, startling her. He whispered "I'm Agent Bob Handy." She whispered back, "You sure are!"

When he released her, Pierce said, "Bob, so nice to see you again. How's your wife Candy and your kids Mandy and Randy?" He frowned at her but recovered with a smile. "Here, the car's this way."

As they got in the car, Bob said, "Sorry if I was too forward, Agent Pierce. The folks in this town know I'm an FBI agent but we can't let the public know that other FBI agents are gathering in Butte. People will talk and that could jeopardize the investigation."

'That's fine, Agent Feely, I mean Handy. Not a problem" said Pierce.

While he drove them to the Butte FBI Field Office, Handy updated them on what information had been gathered. He ushered them into a conference room. Six men seated at the table looked up. Handy gestured at the women, "These are Special Agents Roley and Pierce. They're here with a lead on the Math Bomber case." While the men introduced themselves, Pierce and Roley took seats at one end of the table. Handy loaded a slide carousel into a projector and handed the controller and a list of the slides to Roley. He lowered shades over the windows.

Roley said, "Thank you, Agent Handy, for creating this presentation so quickly, while Agent Pierce and I were en route." She clicked the first slide up onto the screen. Carl Frikes driver's license appeared."We have strong evidence that the Math Bomber is Carl Frikes, a science teacher at Butte High School. The evidence comes from the recent bombing in a storeroom at the NASA Operations Building in Florida. It has been determined that the bomb was disguised as a student science experiment submitted to NASA, to be flown and tested in the Skylab space station."

One agent raised his hand and said, "But that space mission is ongoing. Why was the bomb in a storeroom and not up in the station?"

Pierce chimed in, "Oh but it is." There were gasps. "The high schools involved had to submit two copies of their experiments, one to be flown and one to be used by engineers on the ground to advise the astronaut. The one in space has not exploded, as far as we know. NASA and the astronaut are dealing with it."

Roley held up her hands. "Our focus here has to be entirely on apprehending the Math Bomber. Normally this would mean surveillance of Carl Frikes, building a case for a search warrant of the school and his house. But we also have evidence that Frikes is actually this man."

She clicked to the next slide, a mug shot of Ted, taken when he was arrested for his first bomb in 1969. He looked younger and angrier than in his driver's license photo but still recognizable.

"The suspect was thought to have died in an explosion and fire at Milan Federal Prison in Michigan but we recently found evidence that he had faked his death, escaped, and created a new identity as Carl Frikes. Since he is an escaped felon, there is no need to gather evidence for a search warrant and we can move to apprehend him," Roley said.

She clicked to the next slide, of a document. "This is the Montana registration for the suspect's
Ford Fairlane, license plate number THX1138."

Agent Handy said, "But Montana plates have six characters."

Pierce said, "Yes, it's a vanity plate. Apparently the suspect has a warped sense of humor. *THX1138* is a science fiction movie about a dystopia where humanity lives underground. A charming vision of the future."

Next slide. "And this map shows the location of his house at 2718 Euler, in Butte."

Pierce said. "The high school is in session right now.

Obviously, we don't want to apprehend him there and possibly endanger students. I propose we station agents near his home, in case he's taken the day off for some reason, and another set to the school parking lot. If and when they report that the suspect is leaving the school, they will follow him. If he goes to his home, we converge there and arrest him before he enters the house. If he goes elsewhere, we confer by radio and adjust the plan. Agreed?" she said.

The agents all nodded. Agent Handy said, "I suggest Agent Pierce and I go to the school parking lot. If anyone questions us, she can be a friend new to the area and checking out the school for her kid."

#

Handy and Pierce cruised around the parking lot of the school. "I'm not seeing his car. I don't think he's here," said Handy.

"He might be. He's a super-environmentalist; he may bike to work," said Pierce.

Handy checked by radio with other agents "His car is not outside his house. There's no garage."

Pierce said, "Let's go talk to the Principal." Handy nodded.

#

"Yes, Mr. Norsworthy, my son Randy is really into science," said Pierce.

"Especially space science," chimed in Handy, "Some of your students have an experiment up in the Skylab space station right now, don't they?"

Principal Norsworthy beamed. "Yes, we're very proud of them."

"Is it possible for me to meet the science teacher?" said Pierce. She saw Handy's eyes widen in alarm.

Norsworthy looked apologetic. "Mr. Frikes seems to have taken some sick time off right now."

"Seems to?" Pierce said.

"Yes," Norsworthy said, "He left school suddenly yesterday and hasn't called in. I think I'll stop in at his house after school, to see….".

Pierce was standing. "Let's go Bob." She headed for their car, Handy running to keep up..

#

Luke was suited up and crawling over the outside of the station. He had the electrodynamic tether package strapped to his back, He reached a small port, near the center of mass of the huge station, where he had already installed an electrical connection. This would feed power from the Solar Telescope Mount solar panels. He made sure the tether was strongly secured to the station and carefully uncoiled it, as he had for the Soyuz meal delivery service. The three hundred foot cable stretched away from the station, carrying the electron emitter at its end closer to Earth. Luke returned to the station interior. He removed his helmet and gloves but kept the suit on.

"Hans?"

"Yes Luke, I'm here. Ready to try the system. Over"

"OK, let's start at low power," said Luke, "I don't want to fry the cable or the elcctron emitter." He set the power to the cable at the lowest level possible.

"We're getting a signal from the tether package. Seems A-OK" said Hans, "Try doubling the power. Over."

"Hans, tell me again how much power the design will permit. I'm not going to play with my one chance just to see what happens," said Luke. He tried to keep the tension out of his voice.

"The system should be able to take ten times power level one."

"Should. Fine, I'm amping it up to level two."

An hour later, ground tracking stations verified that Skylab's orbit was dropping slowly. Lukc increased the power to level four, then five. Hans and other physicists at NASA ran computer simulations over and over.

"Luke, with help from the Attitude Engines, you should reach the Russian space station in five days. With the rescue flight two weeks after that. Over," said Hans.

"Five days," Luke said, "OK. Let's hope I can keep the damned centrifuge going that long. Over."

#

Ted pulled off the highway and turned down a small dirt road. There was no traffic and no houses. He opened the trunk and pulled out a screwdriver and a license plate he had taken from a late-model car in a junkyard. He swapped it with the plate on his car. Rummaging through his bug-out bag, he pulled out a pair of manual hair clippers. Using the car's side mirror, he awkwardly gave himself a bad crew cut. He ran his hand over his scalp. He closed his eyes and shuddered as he remembered getting his hair cut off in prison. He pulled himself together. He felt loose hairs scratching his neck. *Damn, I should have remembered a towel.* He got back on the highway.

#

The FBI agent finished taking Althea's statement. He said, "Doctor Nespla, it's very important you not discuss your experience or any discussions or conclusions with anybody."

Althea said, "It's a bit late for that, isn't it? The whole Team and half of NASA knows what happened."

The agent said, "We can't let any further information leak that might help any suspect evade capture. Everyone else here has been given the same warning."

"But the press knows about the explosion and Peter's injury. It's all over TV," she said.

"Yes, that's unfortunate. But we have to prevent any further leaks."

Her phone rang. It was Harry.

"Althea, are you OK? I saw the news."

Althea hesitated. What could she say? "I'm fine, Harry. Luke is alright, too. But I can't really say any more. I'm sorry."

Silence for a few beats.

"OK, thanks Althea. Take care," said Harry. He hung up.

The agent nodded approvingly.

Damn it, thought Althea, *have I pushed Harry farther away? Is he upset with me now? Damn it.*

#

Harry sat at his desk quietly, filled with gratitude toward Althea. He had awoken that morning with an insight and Althea had just given him a valuable bit of information. His mind spun furiously. The FBI must have already interviewed her and issued a gag order. But why would Althea say "Luke is alright too" when questioned about a bomb on the ground at NASA? The news reports were that a bomb had gone off in a storeroom at the Operations Building. That seemed like an odd target for the Math Bomber. But Harry was following the mission closely and knew that some student experiments were on Skylab with copies stored at NASA. Harry had been the one to recruit Peter, the engineer who had been injured by the bomb. He knew Peter was in charge of those experiments. So what if one of the experiments, which each came in matched sets. was actually a bomb? So two bombs, one at NASA, one up with Luke. That would explain why Althea mentioned Luke. So why wasn't he dead? Luke had defused Ted's first bomb years earlier. Maybe the NASA bomb exploded but the station bomb timer lagged a bit, and Luke was warned soon enough to somehow defuse it. So he was 'alright', as Althea said.

Harry pulled out a thick file folder he had made about the Skylab 5 mission. Harry didn't work for NASA but he was obsessed with details and through various channels, some a bit, one might say, informal, he had gathered lots of specifics on the mission. He found the list of student experiments. Twelve of them, submitted from six different states. Looking at the descriptions, he was able to scratch off four that would have required lots of handling by Luke to perform tests. If one of those was a bomb, it would have been discovered or detonated early in the mission. Each experiment on the list included the name of the teacher submitting it. Three of the teachers on the list were women. That left five. One must be Ted. Had to be.

Harry assumed that the FBI was already converging on

those teachers. If Ted had seen the news he'd make the same conclusion and so was on the run. But maybe the FBI hadn't had the same epiphany that Harry had that morning. Harry wondered if he should call Agent Roley or Pierce.

No. I want Ted. I want him to suffer, Harry thought. *The FBI can wait.*

Harry knew he might be accused of interfering with the case but he didn't give a damn. He had five teachers to investigate. He called the first school on the list and got the secretary in the Principal's office. "Hello, I'm Elijah Baley," Harry said, "I'm a writer at *Science News* and I'm working on an article about teachers and space."

"Oh, like our science teacher, Mr. Clement?" she said, "You know, his students actually have a project on the Skylab space station."

"Yes, that's why I called you. But to polish up my article I need to get a bit more information, just to clear up a few minor loose ends. There's no need to bother Mr. Clement. I don't even know if my editors are going to run the article and I don't want to get Mr. Clement's hopes up."

"I understand. What would you like to know?"

"Well first, how long has Mr. Clement been at your school?"

"Oh, he's taught here for years, at least ten I think/"

"I see. And might you know where he's originally from?"

"Born and raised here in San Diego."

Harry thanked her and hung up. Soon he had called all but one school and none of those teachers could be Ted. Harry assumed that if Ted had stolen an identity soon after he escaped a Michigan prison, it would be from someone born in Michigan. So far, the teachers Harry had checked had either been at their school before Ted's escape from prison or were not Michiganders. The last one on the list had to be Ted. Harry's hand shook as he called the school. He couldn't blow this. What if Ted wasn't on the run? Harry couldn't somehow accidentally warn Ted and help him escape again. Overcome with doubt, he hung up before the call was answered. Shaking and breathing hard, he sat in his office. The same office his father Mike Remains had been killed in. The office that had been cleaned, repaired and returned to its original wood-paneled condition. But it would never be the same. Harry missed his Dad so much. What would Dad do now? Harry took a deep breath and picked up the phone.

#

In a gas station bathroom, Ted put on a denim cut-off jacket covered with patriotic slogans and patches. People would notice those and not him. He stopped at a supermarket and got lots of canned goods and other staples. He drove another hour then left the highway. He entered a forest, driving slowly down barely-visible old logging roads. The sun was setting when he reached his little cabin. He hid the car under a tarp and went into the cabin to sleep, safe at last.

#

Harry said to the school clerk, "Thank you. Thank you very much." He hung up. Ted was Carl Frikes of Butte, Montana. Harry thought about the insight he had woken up with that morning. Ted had killed a man to escape from prison. He must have used cash from the man's wallet to live on while he got a new identity and a job. But what else could he get from the wallet? A driver's license. Harry pulled out another file, one on Ted's escape from prison. When Corbin had disappeared, supposedly while on a solo fishing trip vacation, the police had distributed photos of him to help in the search. Harry looked at the photos and thought that, if you squinted a bit, Corbin could pass for Ted. Or rather, Ted could pass for Corbin. Harry called a real estate agent he had worked with. The man had made a fortune in commissions from Harry and owed him. "Jack, Harry Remains here. I need a favor from you."

"Sure Harry, what can I do for you?"

"I need to know if a man named Michael Corbin C-O-R-B-I-N has purchased real estate anywhere in the US in the last two years. How would we go about discretely finding that out?"

"Wow, that's a tall order. We'd have to contact every county in the country and see if there were any title transfers to his name. I think there's more than three thousand counties in the US."

159

"OK," Harry said, "Why don't we start with Montana?"

"That would make it a lot easier, yes."

"And if you find nothing there, try Idaho next. Then Wyoming and Washington. And Jack, I need this done ASAP, today would be great."

"My staff and I will start making calls right away. I'll call you this afternoon with an update."

#

"Montana," Jack said, hours later. "Specifically, a small lot in the Lolo National Forest, in Mineral County, Montana."

"Can a person buy land in a National Forest?" asked Harry.

Jack said, "Some forests include private parcels that existed before the forest was designated that way. The plan is to eventually absorb those parcels into the Federal system but, yes, you can still sometimes buy them."

"How much documentation would you need to transfer the title? Would a driver's license do?" asked Harry.

"Well, this lot was sold to Corbin through a land contract and those can be pretty informal, so yeah, maybe." Jack gave Harry a contact at the county office in Thompson Falls, Montana in case he wanted more info.

"Great work, Jack. Thank you, I appreciate it," Harry said. He hung up and leaned back in his leather chair in his office in The Lucky Leprechaun.

Time for a hike in the woods.

Chapter 34: Countdown

Tuesday morning

Luke circled Friday on the paper calendar he had made to track preparations for the move. Three days and a few hours to go until he would transfer to the currently unmanned Salyut 4 station. Luke knew he was flying Skylab there but had never felt less like a pilot. *'Flying' is just strong a word*, he thought. *Managed drifting? Gentle nudging?* The electrodynamic tether hanging down from Skylab was exerting just a few pounds of force on the massive space station as the tether pushed against the Earth's magnetic field. Luke was used to being in complete and instant control of a jet plane, where his life dependedon his own split-second decisions. Now his life was in the hands of NASA and Team engineers running orbital software. They would call him at all hours to make carefully-timed tiny tweaks in Skylab's orbit, using the small attitude control thrusters.

Otherwise he spent his time caring for the plants, chickens, and rabbits, packing for the move, and running student experiments. Except for the deadly one nestled inside the spinning centrifuge. *Sorry, Butte Montana High School, your experiment is a definite failure. Maybe next time.*

Tuesday evening

Luke took another stab at repairing a failed centrifuge motor. He had already installed the last spare. Three motors drove the big spinning wheel and poor Peter had told him, before Luke launched, that one motor would be enough to keep it going. Luke had his doubts. With a motor failing every few weeks, Luke had to assume putting the full burden on just one or even two motors would kill them even faster. Luke read the label on the failed unit: Tates Motor Company. *When I get home, I'll suggest a new company motto: He Who Has a Tates is Lost.* Usually he would find his own bad jokes a bit of a stress relief. Not this time. He was scared, plain and simple. He sighed. *Man, tough audience.* He reached for tools to open the motor.

Wednesday morning

Rachel saw Althea hang up her desk phone and slump in her chair. Rachel walked over and put a hand on her shoulder. "Hey hun, are you OK?"

Althea looked up, her face drawn with stress. "No, not so much. I just heard from Howard's doctor that he's taken a turn for the worse. He's asking for me. The doctor doesn't think he has much time left."

"What are you going to do?" asked Rachel.

"Talk to Deke and book a flight. I'll have to tell Luke first. I hate to leave until we get him home safely but ..."

"Althea...". Rachel hesitated.

"What?"

"OK, this is awkward but I'm really curious," said Rachel. "I know Mr. Hughes and you and Luke share a real vision of humans in space. Heck, the whole Team does. But, just from reading about him, I always had the impression that Mr. Hughes was, well.."

"Racist?"

Rachel flushed. Althea smiled wanly. "Yeah, he is."

"Then why do you care so much about him? That sounds awful, doesn't it?"

"He and I were kidnapped together in Nicaragua a few years ago. He needed a lot of care and we spent much of the time talking. He always treated me kindly, maybe because it's not so hard for an old white man to accept a black woman caregiver. I won't go into details but, even being a billionaire, he's had a hard life. I think he's changed quite a bit in the last few years and, for whatever racist crap he has left, I forgive him." Althea stood up. "Gotta go Rachel."

#

"Give my best to Howard. Let him know how grateful we are," said Luke. Althea was alone in the small conference room watching Luke on the monitor, floating in zero gravity.

"Flyboy, would you hold up your right hand?" He did.

"Move a little closer to the camera and an inch to your right?" she said. He moved a bit, She put her palm on the screen, over his hand. The camera on her end was set up all wrong for this, she knew. "I've got my hand over yours," she said, tears rolling down her cheeks. He held his hand to hers and smiled gently.

"I love you darlin'. I'll be home soon. Deke and the Team won't let us down. Well, 'down' is what we want, but you know what I mean."

She laughed and shook her head. "God, what I put up with." He blew her a kiss. They hung up.

Wednesday afternoon

Althea sat with Howard's doctor at the Xanadu Hotel. "The pancreatic cancer has spread even further. He refuses chemotherapy but has accepted pain killers. He could expire at any time. I think seeing you may allow him to let go."

Althea nodded. She entered Howard's suite. It smelled like sickness. Howard was in a hospital bed watching a film projected on a wall-screen. Althea recognized it as *Destination Moon*, based on a Heinlein story about a first private mission to the Moon. Howard turned to look at her. He had lost a lot of weight since she had seen him last. He looked like the gaunt old man she had rescued from earthquake rubble years ago. This saddened her, as if all her help since then amounted to nothing.

"Althea!" He smiled and reached a hand out to her. She took it and nodded toward the screen.

"You used to make movies. So what do you think of this one?" she asked.

Howard's voice was faint and breathy, nothing like that of the alpha-male executive he had once been. "For 1950 science fiction, it's not bad. The acting is a little wooden but the writing is tight. Beautiful background art by Bonestell." The movie closed with "This is THE END …. of the Beginning". Althea moved to turn off the projector. She opened the window shades a crack, to lighten the room just a bit, and returned to sit next to Howard.

"Are you watching a space rescue movie because of Luke?"

Howard turned pained eyes toward her. It seemed to her that the pain came from guilt, not illness. "Yes, I've been thinking of him, and you, a lot. I have to confess something to you, Doc."

"You don't need…"

"No! I have to!" Howard insisted. He paused, coughing. "I was reading about King David, in the Bible you know. Maybe I'm finding religion, heh! Anyway, he was quite a jerk. He sent a husband into battle because he coveted the man's wife. Well, I am so sorry Doc but I'm just as bad. I sent Luke up to Skylab, all alone." His eyes teared up. "I realized later that maybe I did that because I was jealous of him. I wanted you all to myself."

Althea squeezed his hand and said, "Who wouldn't?" Howard barked a laugh.

"Really, Howard, Luke is a big boy. And a smart one. He wanted to go on this mission and I trust him to get home safe. By the way, he wanted me to tell you how grateful he is to you. We all are. But he'll come see you after he lands and tell you himself."

Howard snorted. "Bullshit, Doc, as you might say. My little red wagon's front wheels are over the cliff edge. I'll be gone before that big lug gets back. You and he and Harry are going to have to carry on our grand plan of humans living in space without me. Promise me you'll do that?"

"Yes, Howard, we will."

"Oh hey, and scatter my ashes on the Moon? That would be nice."

She held his hand, talking quietly about this and that. When he dozed off, she gently let go and left the room quietly. She said goodbye to the doctor. As the
elevator doors closed, she began crying.

Thursday morning

Try as he might, Luke could not get the failed motors to function smoothly in tests. The bearings were shot and he had no replacements. But he did learn something useful: once a motor started to squeak and fail, it was close to seizing up. If it was mounted to the centrifuge when that happened it would act like a brake, overload the remaining motors, stop the centrifuge, and then… Yeah, he had to stay on top of removing squeakers. Good to know.

Thursday afternoon

"So Comrade Priss," said Commander Pyotr Klimuk, "The hatch on the Apollo Command Module and the hatch on our Salyut 4 station are not compatible. Your 'Team' and our engineers discussed making an adaptor to join them but decided there was not enough time to test it or train your rescue crew to dock to Salyut 4. So when NASA arrives there in two weeks you will have to spacewalk between the two vessels."

"Understood Pyotyr," said Luke.

"Also, all the documents and control labels in Salyut 4 are obviously in Russian which I know you don't read."

"Or speak," said Luke.

"So I must instruct you now in the minimum you need to know to communicate by radio with us when you are onboard. At that time, I will guide you through whatever else you need to know to run the station," said Pyotr.

"Thank you Comrade."

"It is nothing. When we finally meet, you will buy the first round of drinks."

Thursday night

Luke dreamed that another centrifuge motor was failing. The squealing sound rose to a shriek. Luke bolted awake. It wasn't a dream. He leaped to the centrifuge and fumbled for his tools. Quickly, he removed the bad motor before it could seize up. It was hot from the friction of failed bearings and he burned his fingers. He floated near the centrifuge, panting with fear. The two remaining motors seemed to be operating OK. He checked the centrifuge rotation speed: unchanged. Luke got some ice to sooth his fingers and then tried to get back to sleep.

Friday morning

"Ground Control calling Skylab 5. Do you read me?" Luke woke up to Deke's voice just before his alarm went off. He was bleary-eyed but surprised and glad he had gotten a bit more sleep. Today was going to be a busy day. The centrifuge ticked away and the chickens clucked quietly.

"I read you Control. Over."

"Big day, Luke. Rendezvous in four hours."

"I'll be ready."

"Luke, regarding your desire to transfer the livestock, as you call the rabbits and chickens, to Salyut 4, we think it's too risky. You will be transporting experiments and stored biological samples...."

Frozen eggs, chicks, and bunnies, thought Luke.

"... and including the living test subjects will make it all too cumbersome," said Deke.

"I hear you Control. On the other hand, I am determined to complete the mission as best I can. That means returning with as much data and samples as possible. Let's compromise. If I conclude Salyut 4 is passing me at too great a distance, I will immediately abandon the test subjects to their fate. My call."

Silence for a few beats.

"All right Luke. Your call."

"Thanks Deke, I'll be careful."

Ninety minutes to rendezvous

Luke donned his suit and carried the Manned Maneuvering Unit into the airlock. He made sure the compressed gas tank on the jet-backpack was full and strapped on a spare tank for good measure. He exited the airlock and clipped the MMU to the outside of Skylab. He would strap himself into the MMU when it was time to transfer to Salyut 4. As he turned to go back into Skylab, he saw the Soviet station pass by, maybe four hundred feet away. His heart pounded. Had there been a mistake? Was he missing his one chance for escape?

"Skylab 5 calling Control. Do you read me?"

"Control here Luke," said Deke.

"Control, I think I know the answer to this but please, please tell me I'm right. Salyut 4 just passed by. I didn't miss my bus, did I?"

"No Luke, you didn't. Sorry we didn't warn you but Salyut 4 will be closest to you after one more orbit. In eighty one minutes."

"Whew! Thought so, OK, good. I'll be ready."

Luke entered the station and finished packing. The last and weirdest part was dealing with the rabbits and chickens. When they had been brought to Skylab, they were in cages and moved straight from the pressurized space capsule to the pressurized station. Now they were going to pass through the vacuum of space, something the Team had not planned for.

Luke's solution was to use the spacesuits left by the previous crews. All the living baby bunnies went into one cage which just fit in the torso of Gibson's spacesuit. With no room for more cages, he gently put the four rabbits into the arms and legs of the suit and clamped on the helmet. He made sure air was circulating through the suit from tanks on its back. He did the same for the chickens and chicks.

Gregory Peck protested and fluttering wildly, broke from his grasp. She flew down the station, heading for the centrifuge. Luke shoved off the wall and managed to snag her before she reached it. He narrowly avoided crashing into it himself. *God, I hate chickens*, he thought. He returned to Carr's spacesuit and stuffed Gregory into it, clamping down the helmet. She climbed into view, squawking furiously at him through the visor. In the inflated suit, she looked like an alien in a low-budget science fiction film. *A Cockwork Orange?*

Luke moved the bundle of experiments, cases of biological samples, collapsed animal cages, and feed bags, all wrapped together with duct tape, to the outside of the station. Then he transferred both spacesuits full of critters outside as well. He decided he had time for one last look and went into the station.

Thank you Skylab. Good job.

One of the two motors on the centrifuge started squealing.

Luke thought he had enough time to pull it and he started moving to do that. Then the sound changed. A weird harmonic. As he came up to the centrifuge he realized *Oh shit. The last motor is failing too.* The centrifuge slowed.

He scrambled to change direction, crashing into the wall of the station, yanking on handholds with frantic strength, trying to reach the airlock.

#

Althea sat at her station at NASA, watching Luke's life signs readouts. His respiration and heart rate were spiking. Then nothing. *Hmm.. maybe he's knocked his sensors off again?* She thought. Engineers were shouting at Deke. Her heart sank.

Chapter 35: Lost in Space

"Mr. Remains, we are landing at Thompson Falls Airport in five minutes," said the pilot over the PA. Harry gathered his carry-on bag and the special package. He looked around the cabin. This was the same jet that he and Luke had flown in to Nicaragua to rescue Althea. Now it belonged to Howard Hughes but as the manager of Hughes' casinos, Harry had the use of it. And he was using it to stop Ted. *Kind of the opposite of a rescue,* he mused.

He tried to feel nostalgic about the plane but couldn't. It was just a tool. Everything lately was a tool, to be used to reach goals. *I used to have fun,* he thought. Harry tried to think of the last time he had been impulsive, done a silly thing just for the fun of it. Maybe six years before, when he, Althea, and Luke were at the World Science Fiction Convention in '69.

At the costume ball Althea had been dressed as a Medical Officer from the Starship Enterprise. Harry remembered her getting pissed at people who thought she was Uhura. "No, she wore red, my uniform is blue. She was Communications Officer, I'm in Medical," she would explain, less and less patiently as the night went on. "Oh, so you're a black Nurse Chapel?" they might respond. "Dammit, I'm a doctor, not a nurse. Do you really think it's reasonable that a starship crew of four hundred and thirty would have just one doctor on board?" she would fire back. Luke and Harry had to drag her away from a few heated discussions.

Luke had been dressed as Doc Savage, the Man of Bronze, hero of pulp adventure stories from the 30's and 40s. For some reason, Doc Savage was usually depicted wearing a tattered shirt, as if his combat with villains destroyed his wardrobe but not his rippling muscles.

"Are those stories even science fiction? You just like showing off your nice pecs," Althea had said.

"Nice?" Luke had asked.

Althea laid a hand on his chest. "Very nice."

Harry remembered feeling a tap on his shoulder and turning to see a cute little redhead dressed as a fairy.

"And who are you supposed to be?" she had said.

"I'm Hari Seldon, creator of the Foundation," spreading his arms to display his finery.

Sharon, as he came to know her, looked skeptical. "You're just wearing a suit. A kinda futuristic suit but still.."

"Yes, it's very subtle. Like Seldon's psychohistory calculations," Harry had said. He remembered spending the rest of the night with Sharon. *I should really look her up*, he thought. *If I survive this little trip.*

#

Luke flew into the airlock, crashing into the far wall, as the screeching motors on the centrifuge reached a crescendo. He slammed the inside hatch shut and scrambled out of the station. As he fumbled with a clip, trying to secure himself, the walls of the workshop ruptured and the air blew out, shoving the entire station toward him. The airlock hatch crashed into him. Adrenaline slowed time down to a crawl. Luke noted, in a detached way, that in the vacuum of space he had heard nothing as the bomb went off. He was bounced off the hatch and flung away from Skylab. As he passed the secured space-suited critters, he flailed and twisted, trying to grab hold of Gregory Peck's inflated glove. He missed by inches and watched Skylab slowly recede.

#

Harry stepped off the plane and surveyed the small airstrip with hangers and offices a long walk away. Mountains, pine trees, and blue sky surrounded the airport. The pilot stuck his head out the hatch. "Mr. Remains, I'll prep the plane for your return to Las Vegas. Can you tell me when that might be?" Harry watched a white pickup truck crossing the field toward the plane.

"Return without me, as soon as you're ready. I'm not sure how long this will take. I'll call you when I need a ride back."

The pickup pulled up next to the plane and a young woman stepped out.

"Mr. Remains?" she asked.

"Yes but you can call me Harry. Are you the clerk from the County office?"

171

"Yep. I'm Helen Wheels. You can call me Ms. Wheels."

Harry smiled. *Not impressed by the rich guy in his private jet, eh?*

"Ms. Wheels, can we go back to your office and talk?" said Harry.

"Before we do, Harry, I'd like to clear something up. When your guy called the County office and asked me to search our files for a land purchase and, later, to help you when you came here, he offered me $200 for my trouble." She waited patiently and a little skeptically.

Harry pulled out his wallet and counted out two hundred. That seemed to impress Ms. Wheels more than the jet. "Let's go," she said, climbing into the pickup. Harry waved goodbye to the watching pilot.

#

"Quiet!" shouted Deke. The clamor in the Control room stopped. Althea saw him glance at her. She sat silently at her station with her arms crossed. No hysterics. She was an Emergency Room doctor letting him handle this emergency. She felt Rachel and Billie standing close to her.

"All right," Deke said, "We've lost radio contact with Skylab. No telemetry either. We must assume the bomb has gone off." Murmurs. "Quiet!"

Deke went to stand below the big display showing the orbital paths of Skylab and the Russian Salyut 4 station. They overlapped.

"We must also assume that Commander Priss has left Skylab and is about to move toward the Salyut station. We no longer can communicate with him since the systems on Skylab have shut down...."

Althea's mind was racing, trying to stay calm. She had enough presence to think *Shut down? That's like saying an exploding rocket has 'undergone rapid disassembly'.* She tried to keep the images of Peter and the carnage in the storeroom out of her mind.

".. so we will link up with the Soviet Ground Control. They can let us know if, when Commander Priss enters Salyut 4 and tie him into our communications."

\#

Luke drifted farther from Skylab. Not quickly but that didn't matter. He was not in the Manned Maneuvering Unit jetpack and so had no way to move one foot closer to Skylab, let alone a hundred feet. He certainly couldn't get to the Salyut station. *Should I be resigning myself to death right about now?* He chewed on that for a second. *Screw that.*

In the time-honored tradition of engineers, 'Change Something and See What Happens', Luke windmilled an arm around a few times which rotated him to face a different direction. He saw the end of the slack electrodynamic tether floating four feet away. Just out of reach. Luke groped around his suit frantically until he found the short cable he had tried, and failed, to use to tie himself to the outside of Skylab. He managed to unclip it from his waist. *Don't drop it. Don't drop it,* he prayed. Clutching one end of the short steel cable, he swung it toward the tether. Missed. He stretched as far as his spacesuit would allow and tried again. Missed by inches. The cable just wasn't long enough. *OK. All-or-nothing time.*

Using all his strength, Luke threw the cable away.

\#

Cosmonaut Pyotr Klimuk stood before his commander. "Sir, the American astronaut on Skylab is in grave danger. The Outer Space Treaty requires that we assist any distressed crew in space, whatever their nation, if possible. We have a Proton rocket and Soyuz capsule available…"

His superior raised a hand. Pyotr fell silent.

"Colonel, as I have already told the Americans, we cannot prepare a ship any faster than they can. We will leave any rescue to them. They canceled the Soyuz/Apollo mission abruptly and without consulting us. We will not change any more missions just to suit them."

Pyotr was about to protest but saw that his commander was resolute.

"Yes, sir."

His commander nodded and bent over his paperwork. He noticed that Pyotr was still there.

"Was there something else, colonel?"

"Yes sir. I know the next project is an unmanned mission but I wonder if I might be assigned to it, perhaps in an advisory role? I have the time and I may be able to suggest improvements, based on my experience in space."

His superior peered at him.

"There is no glory to be had in that project. Why…"

"Just to keep my hand in, sir. Working with technicians on the ground may teach me useful things for future missions." The commander waved a hand at him.

"Fine. I will inform Kozlov that you are assigned to his project."

"Thank you, sir."

Chapter 36: The Gripping Hand

The short steel cable weighed maybe a pound, a tiny fraction of Luke's mass. So when Luke threw the cable away behind him as hard as he could, it very gently pushed him in the opposite direction. Slowly he drew closer to the end of the limp electrodynamic tether. Agonizing seconds passed. Finally, he could reach out and snag the tether. Elation flooded his chest. But he had no time to waste. He passed the tether through his hands until it drew taut. Thanking the gods that the explosion had not severed the tether from Skylab, Luke pulled himself hand over hand back toward the ruined station. He picked up speed and, though his fear made him want to keep pulling, he didn't want to crash into the station. So he forced himself to simply let his momentum carry him closer. The station grew larger. He didn't want to hit it headfirst so he windmilled an arm to turn his feet around. When he struck the station, moving too damn fast, the thin aluminum wall flexed inward alarmingly. It no longer had air pressure inside keeping it stiff.

Luke grabbed a handhold. Though the bomb had killed the station, turning it into eighty tons of scrap, he felt a wave of relief as if he were safe. As if. In reality, getting to the Russian station was his only hope. Sliding one hand along the tether, never releasing his only lifeline, he crawled as fast as he could around the outside of Skylab. He found the bundle of experiment samples and two space suits full of critters waiting for him. Gregory Peck glared at him accusingly through her visor.

Luke hurriedly climbed into the frame of the MMU jetpack. This made him feel secure enough that he could use a jagged edge of metal on the ruptured wall of the station to saw through the tether, freeing it from the station. He tied that end of the tether around the two spacesuits and bundle and rapidly coiled up the rest. When he found the other end, he knotted it to the jetpack frame., Then he unclipped the critters from the station, and shoved them out into space away from Skylab and, he hoped, in the direction of the Salyut station. Strapping them to the jetpack would have made it all too awkward and unbalanced. The tether between them gave him room to maneuver.

Luke peered in the direction he thought the Salyut station would be approaching from. Nothing. He checked his watch. Based on his last check with Ground Control, Salyut should pass in ninety seconds. It should be just visible by now. Maybe the explosion and release of air from Skylab had turned the station and he was looking in the wrong direction? He had no time to scramble around the curve of Skylab and look around. He had to get some distance away so Skylab didn't block his view so much. Luke pressed triggers on the hand controls and nitrogen gas squirted from little thrusters. He moved out in the same direction as the spacesuited chickens and bunnies.

#

Althea watched Deke pacing the Control Room, waiting for the Soviets to respond with any word about Luke. The Team clustered around Althea. She swiveled in her chair to face them.

"I'm sure he's fine," said Rachel. Others made comforting sounds as well.

Althea held up a hand to silence them.

"Please. Stop. I know you mean well and I thank you. But I would rather we focus on Luke and anything that might help him."

Hans said, "Unless... until he reaches the Soyuz station, there's nothing we can do."

"Hans!" scolded Rachel.

Althea shook her head. "Not quite true, Hans. We can keep looking at the info the Soviets sent us on the Soyuz station and try to anticipate any problems he might have there."

Hans gazed at her for a few beats. He nodded. "You're right, of course. Let's go back to the office and do that." The Team members started to head back but Althea remained at her post.

"I need to stay for a bit," she said.

Billy looked at her as if to say *need company?* Althea shook her head and shooed them all away.

#

When the rest of the Team entered the office, Hans looked at the clock and said, "Assuming Luke is still alive, his spacesuit air supply will run out in less than two hours."

Billy slammed the Soyuz folder on her desk. "Then we damn well better be ready with some brilliant advice when we hear from him."

#

Luke used the jetpack thrusters to slowly spin, so he could search the whole sky for the approaching Soviet station. Nothing. He checked his watch, his heart pounding. It should be here, right about…

The Soyuz station emerged from behind Skylab.   Luke immediately stopped his spin and jetted to intercept it. He passed the experiment sample bundle and two spacesuits of livestock. The station loomed up, smaller than Skylab but blessedly intact. He tapped the left thruster. His speed and angle were perfect. He would gently 'land' on the station just near the airlock. *Damn, you're good,* he thought. Luke reached out to grasp the base of an antenna projecting from the station. His head snapped forward as he was jerked back. He watched in horror as Salyut moved away from him.

#

"Coffee?" Helen Wheels said.

"Yes, please," said Harry. She poured them each a cup from an old percolator.

"Sorry, I'm out of cream and sugar."

Harry took that to mean that she took her coffee unsweetened and black and rarely had visitors. Helen leaned back in her swivel chair behind her desk in the County office. Harry sat in the flimsy plastic guest chair.

"So Harry, why are you interested in a little one acre lot in the middle of a national forest?"

Harry had to choose his words carefully. Helen was sharp and if he bullshitted too much, she would pick that up and stop cooperating. He needed her to cooperate. But if he told her the whole truth, she would call in the local sheriff and Harry wanted Ted all to himself.

"Ms. Wheels, when my agent called you to ask if a Michael Corbin had registered a deed in your county, he was obviously looking for Corbin, not a particular property."

"OK Harry, then why the interest in Corbin?" Helen smiled and Harry could see she knew she was being cheeky with the rich guy from Las Vegas. She was having fun.

"I became a lawyer, Ms. Wheels, ..," Harry began. He saw her stiffen and thought, *And like many non-lawyers, you're happy to be judge, jury, and executioner of us.* But he said. "..mostly to help my family with their Mom-and-Pop casino and hotel in Las Vegas." She relaxed a bit. "But I'm also the executor of my father's estate. He died last year."

"Oh, I'm sorry, Harry."

"Thanks. It's taken all this time for me to track down Corbin. If the man in the woods is the right 'Michael Corbin', and not just someone with the same name, I need to deliver this special package to him." Harry patted the box next to him. "I know my father would have wanted me to." And every word was true.

"OK Harry, let's find your dad's friend." Helen had turned to pull some maps from a shelf so she didn't see Harry grimace at her words. She looked at a form on her desk, the record of the deed to the forest plot. She picked one map from the pile and spread it open on the desk.

#

Luke realized that the tether had become taut and the mass of the test samples and spacesuited animals had stopped his movement toward the Salyut station. He hurriedly untied his end of the tether and set them free. *Sorry guys.*

He jetted toward the station again and had almost reached it when the last of the pressurized gas propellant fizzed from the jetpack. *No!*

His heart pounding, Luke quickly unbuckled the jetpack. Useless, it was now a hindrance. He kicked off from it, sending it spinning away. It took only a few seconds but it felt like a day of torture to reach the station. He forced himself to not stretch out his arm. He didn't want to bounce off and then not be able to reach it again. The station slowly glided past him. When he was inches away, he slowly reached out with both gloved hands and grasped the end of one of the three big solar power panels. He closed his eyes and a sense of déjà vu washed through him. Just like when he had managed to return to the ruined Skylab, Luke felt the same relief then urgency. He had to reach an airlock before his suit's tank was empty. He began pulling himself carefully along the edge of the solar panel toward the body of the station. He risked a glance around to see the two spacesuits of livestock drifting away, only a hundred feet or so distant from him but out of reach. He found the airlock entrance to the Soviet station.

#

Deke checked the link to the Soviet Ground Control. "Colonel Klimuk, do you read me? Over."
"Yes, Major Slayton, we are still here," said Pyotr over the speaker system, "No signal yet from Salyut 4. We will let you know the instant we receive one."   When the Soviets had received the request to help Luke make use of their station, the program head had balked but Pyotr convinced him of the good press the Party would receive around the world.
"Thank you, Colonel," said Deke. He glanced at the wall clock then at Althea. One hour of air left for Luke. Althea sighed, got up from her station and came
to him.
"Deke, I'm sorry, I don't want to distract you. I know you're doing what you can. I just have to be here until we know for sure…". He reached for her hand in sympathy.
Pyotr's voice boomed, "Major, something has happened at Salyut 4! We detect a slight, very small, drop in the power level."
Cheers rang out in the Control Room.

#

The light switch was just where Pyotr had told Luke it

would be.

Chapter 37: Way Station

Luke closed the inner airlock hatch. Like Skylab, the inside of Salyut 4 was a long cylinder. But this station was a lot smaller than Skylab, about a fourth its size. Luke took off his gloves and helmet. The station was cold and smelled like a locker room. It was heavenly. Luke was filled with gratitude to the Russians. He was also exhausted. But before he could get out of his suit and collapse, he found the communications panel and contacted the Russians, as Pyotr had instructed him.

"Mission Control Moscow, Skylab 5 here. Do you read me? Over." Luke thought he heard a response but it was drowned out by shouts in Russian and English. "Please repeat. Over."

"Colonel Klimuk here. We read you, Skylab 5. Welcome to Salyut 4. We will pass you to NASA Mission Control now. Over."

Luke knew that NASA and so Althea were listening in and his heart was aching to hear her voice but .. "Wait Pyotr, I need to know something and it can't wait."

"What is it, Skylab 5? Over."

"How do I operate the TACS on Salyut 4?"

"Tacks?"

"Your thruster attitude control system."

"Why must you know that?"

"Pyotr, this is needed to complete my mission. I have to move the station. Not a lot, I hope, but time is critical. Please trust me on this. I don't want to hit random controls and see what happens."

Pyotr was silent. Luke knew his superiors would probably refuse the request until it was too late and that Pyotr would be putting his own career on the line. Luke waited anxiously.

"Skylab 5, I need to know more. Over."

"Pyotr, in order to reach your station I had to cut loose my experiment samples and live animals. They are drifting away as we speak. If I lose them, I will have nothing to show for my mission. But if I can maneuver to reach them… "

Deke Slayton came online. "Lieutenant Priss, this is NASA Ground Control.. Let it go. That's an order. Your mission now is to get home in one piece."

"Beg to differ, Major. I plan to do both. As the only occupant of this ship… *Yeah, if you can maneuver it, let's call it a ship…*I am effectively the Captain and my word is law. Pyotr?"

Luke could hear Pyotr take a deep breath as he committed himself. "Skylab 5, first you must open the covers on the seven station windows, to help you locate your package. Then go to the left seat in front of the main control console, facing the airlock"

Luke hurried to obey. He jumped from one small window to the next until he saw the two spacesuits and bundle, with the slack tether trailing away. He moved to the seat. "All right, Mission Control Moscow, I am in position. I have observed the package, about two hundred meters away and, from my seated orientation, I would say thirty degrees to my right and twenty degrees up."

"Skylab 5, I believe the attitude engines will not be sufficient to reach your objective," said Pyotr.

"Damn it!"

"Indeed. But you will use them to point the station toward your items. Then you must use the main engines to reach them."

"Pyotr, I don't want to crash the station into them."

"So this will require a very fine hand at the controls. The main engines must fire at the lowest power level for the shortest time possible," said Pyotr, "How would you say it? Like a sparrow's fart."

"Sure, that's exactly how I would say it. OK, tell me how."

Luke listened, checked the position of the suits and bundle again through the windows, then tweaked the small attitude rocket engines until the station was pointed the right way.

"Here goes," said Luke as he tapped the controls for the two large rocket engines. The thrust was more of a belch than a fart. Luke jumped to the windows and watched the package drift past. He turned the station and tried again. And again. This time the package passed a hundred feet or so away but, for a few seconds, he thought he heard a faint scraping sound through the walls of the station. Peering through the small windows he saw the suits and bundle hanging motionless. The tether must have snagged on something.

"OK, Moscow Ground Control, I may have caught the package. I'm going to do an EVA to see," said Luke.

Deke Slayton broke in. "Skylab 5, I will remind you that your suit air supply is almost gone."

"Understood. I will be as quick as possible. Althea, if you're listening, I'll be fine. Love you. Over."

Pyotr said, "Skylab 5, you will need safety lines and clips to do your EVA. They are in the center locker."

Luke cursed silently. He had forgotten to ask for those. His fatigue was making him sloppy. He retrieved the lines from the locker.

"Got them. Going out now."

He clamped on his helmet and donned his gloves. Luke exited the station and carefully secured himself to an antenna mast. He searched for the suits and bundle and saw them in the distance hanging at the far end of the tether. The sun in his face was making it hard to locate the other end. Luke moved around the outside of the station slowly, stretching to hook one safety line before unhooking another.   Minutes later, he saw the end of the taut tether snagged around a transponder at the back end of the station. He moved to it and pulled the bundle to him, coiling the tether up. He noted idly that Gregory Peck was no longer visible in the helmet. *Focus!*

He was moving back to the airlock, towing the bundle behind him, when his low air alarm went off.

#

Helen Wheels pointed to a spot on the map spread out on her desk. "This is Corbin's lot."

Harry peered at the map. "How far is it from us?"

"About thirty miles, some of it down pretty rough logging roads. It would take at least an hour to get there. Maybe two."

Harry looked surprised. "I thought Thompson Falls was right in Lolo National Forest."

Helen smiled. The ignorance of city folk could be amusing. "We are. The forest covers more than two million acres." Harry looked at her blankly. She tried again. "More than three thousand square miles? Roughly sixty miles across?"

"Wow," said Harry. He looked at his watch.

"The sun will be close to setting by then. I'd rather visit Mr. Corbin during the day. Is there a nice motel in town?"

"Sure, the Falls Inn. My folks own it. I know they have a vacancy.".

"So Ms. Wheels, can I ask you to point me there? Also, if you'd drive me to Corbin's place tomorrow morning, I'll treat for breakfast and pay you for your trouble. Deal?"

Helen smiled and folded up the map. "Deal, Harry."

#

Luke could feel the flow of air into his helmet dropping off. He fought off panic. *Slow and steady*. He fumbled for the end of a safety line and twisted to reach the next clamping point. The two spacesuits and bundle he towed behind him felt like an anchor. The alarm stopped. So did the air flow. His spacesuit used to feel like a cozy safe haven. Now it was a cloth coffin. His helmet was a window in the coffin so he could see the Universe as he died. Luke was gasping for air and felt an overwhelming urge to take off his helmet. Instead, he forced his hands to move from one handhold to the next.

He reached the airlock. And realized it was too small for him, the critters, and the bundle. His hands shaking, he wrapped the tether around a handhold and left them all outside while he entered the airlock alone. It took forever to cycle and, when he could open the inner hatch, his vision was starting to go black around the edges. He used his last strength to twist his helmet off. Gasping in the cold air, he unzipped his suit and waited for his heart to stop pounding. Then zipped up and put his helmet back on.

The bit of 'fresh' air now in the suit should give him a minute to act. He entered the airlock again and retrieved the spacesuit with the bunnies. Once inside, he opened that suit's helmet and swapped its air tank with the one on his suit. The rabbits had not used nearly as much air as he had. He left them in their suit for now. Two more trips outside and he had everything safely in the Salyut station. He took off his helmet and gloves and went to the console.

"Mission Control NASA and Moscow, Skylab 5 here. Do you read me? Over."

"NASA Mission Control reads you loud and clear, Skylab 5," said Deke, "Did you manage to retrieve your package? Over."

"Affirmative. Everything I could carry out of Skylab is now in Salyut 4. Rabbits and chickens are starting to emerge from their spacesuits. I have to tend to the livestock and then I really need some sleep. Over."

"Hold on a moment, Skylab 5," said Deke. A few seconds passed.

"Hey honey," Althea said. "Over. Roger. Whatever."

Luke felt a wave of longing sweep through him. Longing to be standing on Earth, holding her in his arms, done with this damned mission. But if he were
on Earth right now, he would collapse to the ground in exhaustion. Floating in zero gravity should have felt effortless, a blessing. But, weirdly, he felt cheated. Like he was being given no excuses, no relief. *Keep on keeping on.* Once again, he pulled energy from somewhere.

"Hey darlin', what's new?"

"Peter's getting out of the hospital tomorrow. Your retrieval launch should be ready to go in ten days, on November 16. So you'll be home for Thanksgiving."

"Good, good," Luke said. His thoughts were getting fuzzy with fatigue. "I really miss you darlin'."

Althea said quietly, "I miss you too, honey. Promise me you'll stay as safe as you can. No more adventures, OK?"

"I promise, sweetheart."

"Goodnight flyboy. Sleep well. We'll talk tomorrow. Here's Pyotr."

The cosmonaut came on. "Moscow Mission Control here. Skylab 5, we know you are poopie...."

"Pooped. I think, I hope you mean 'pooped'" said Luke.

"Tired then. But I must review some controls with you before you sleep. Like temperature, air flow, water supply, etc."

After that, Luke turned up the temperature, fastened cages

to walls, put critters in them, set up food and water for the animals, put covers over windows, and finally crawled into a sleeping bag he found. He was out in seconds.

#

Helen picked up Harry outside the motel early the next morning. The day was cold and clear. He was wearing shiny new black boots, a camouflage jacket, cap, and matching pants. Helen grinned. "Sorry Harry, I almost didn't see you there."

"Very funny." He loaded his package and carry on bag into her truck. "Let's get breakfast."

The portions at Minnie's Montana Cafe were huge. When they were served, Harry stared at the eggs, hash browns, sausage, ham, and toast filling his plate and said, "Man, I don't know if I can finish all this."

Helen said, "Eat up Harry. We're going to be doing some hiking today and we'll need the calories."

"I thought we were driving to the site."

"We'll try to get close but, looking at the map, even the bad road runs out some ways from the cabin. I won't drive my truck off road. I'm thinking the cabin builders really wanted to be isolated from the teaming masses in Thompson Falls," Helen said.

"Population 900?" said Harry.

She shrugged. "Some people just really don't like people. Maybe Mr. Corbin is one of those."

Harry nodded. "Yeah, I believe he is."

"But you like people, don't you Harry?"

"I lean that way, yes. I even like you." She stuck her tongue out at him.

Harry gazed at her thoughtfully while she ate. She was small, with her short black hair in some kind of pixie cut. But she carried herself confidently and seemed to take up a larger space.

"Ms. Wheels," Harry said, "I need to go back to the motel before we hit the road. I forgot to do something."

#

The next morning, Luke rearranged the animal cages. Amazingly, all the rabbits and chickens, even the babies, had survived being stuffed into spacesuits and dragged through the vacuum. But the critters were not crazy about being in zero g. So, like he had in Skylab, Luke let the air flowing to the ventilating fan intake pass through the cages and help hold animal waste and feed against pads on the floor of each cage. This reduced debris floating through the station which already smelled like a crowded pet shop.

Luke didn't care. Keeping the animal study going, sort of, felt like giving the finger to the Math Bomber. Luke found that anger against that bastard

was a strong motivation to succeed. And love for Althea was a great reason to survive. He was happy to be alive.

Whistling, he reviewed all the supplies in the station. Did he have enough to last until NASA picked him up in ten days? Food and water were more than adequate, both for him and the critters. There was enough air for twenty days so he was good to go. Luke dug out his microfiche library of science fiction and found 'Sidewise in Time' by Murray Leinster. Luke had a fascination for alternate history stories. He mused a bit. He hated Ted but wondered what would have happened if Ted hadn't put that bomb in the Undergraduate Library? Luke would probably never have met Althea or Harry. Howard Hughes might have died in Nicaragua. And Luke wouldn't be an astronaut trying to survive a bomb from Ted. Luke shook his head and settled in for a good read.

#

Helen drove her truck west on the interstate. Harry and she mostly talked about movies and TV shows. Naturally, Harry brought up science fiction. Helen had seen 'Dark Star', a space comedy. Harry asked, "So what did you think of it?"

"Well, the talking smart bomb was probably the most interesting character, but the movie was fun and silly." She turned onto a two lane gravel road.

Harry really didn't want the conversation to turn to bombs. The FBI had Ted's Wanted posters hanging in post offices across the country. Helen may have seen one and Harry didn't want her thoughts going anywhere in that direction.

"Any other movies you've liked?" he asked.

"'Silent Running' was good," she said, "You know, the one where the Earth's environment is collapsing and they sent all these big spaceships out full of endangered plants and animals? Then the government cancels the program and wants to blow up all the ships?"

Harry nodded warily.

Helen went on, "But I didn't like it when Bruce Dern started to kill off the rest of the crew on his ship. I mean, I could sympathize with his goal to protect the plants and animals that had gone extinct back on Earth but he seemed a little psychotic. More than a little."

Desperate to change the subject, Harry said,   "So, any favorite TV shows growing up? That weren't science fiction?"

"Well, I always liked 'The Fugitive'.with David Janssen. I thought he was dreamy. So romantic, an innocent man running from the police."

Christ, thought Harry.

Helen turned down a narrow dirt road and slowed down, trying to avoid potholes and stumps. Glad for the distracting change, Harry said, "How far do you think the cabin is?"

Helen stopped the truck and consulted the map. "It's about a mile straight south from here. The road runs out about a quarter mile from the cabin. We'll have to walk that last bit."

"No, Ms. Wheels," said Harry.

She cocked her head at him quizzically. "No? What do you mean? I won't try to drive through …"

"I mean that from this point I'll hike in on my own, alone," Harry said.

Helen blinked. She said quietly,"So I'll wait for you here?"

"Actually, no. I really need you to drive back to town, to the motel. I left an envelope for you with your Mom at the front desk. It's very important that you open the envelope, Ms. Wheels." He opened the door, climbed out, and gathered his bag and package.

"What the hell, Harry? How are you going to get back to

town? This makes no sense." Helen looked bewildered and angry.

Harry said, "I'm sorry. I just have to do this on my own. I brought a compass so I should be able to find the main road again. Then I'll hitchhike back."

Helen opened the glove box and pulled out a pistol. Harry's eyes widened.

"Harry, you idiot, at least take this with you. There are bears out here."

"There are?" he gulped.

"Yes. If you meet one, don't run away. Give them a chance to leave first. If you have to shoot, don't aim for the head. They have thick skulls, like yours."

"OK," he said. He gingerly pocketed the gun. Shutting the truck door, Harry said, "Ms. Wheels, again, it's very important that you open the envelope. Also, there's two hundred in it to compensate you for your help today."

"Screw you, Harry." She backed the truck up and spun the tires as she took off back up the road.

Harry sadly watched her go. *I didn't want it to end that way. She might be the last sweet person I ever meet and now she's pissed at me.* He sighed, looked at his watch, checked the direction on his compass, and started down the logging road. The forest was quiet. No traffic noises. Just the wind blowing through the trees and the crunch of his boots on the rough ground. Very peaceful. Harry had to remind himself not to zone out. Every minute, he would pause and look in all directions. After all, there were bears and a mad bomber somewhere nearby. This part of the park was so dense with tall skinny pine trees that you couldn't see very far. Pine needles covered the ground and muffled any sounds. There were occasional big boulders on either side.

Harry stayed on the road so he wouldn't get lost. After thirty minutes of slow walking, he saw another big mass next to the road that looked a bit odd. A boulder? No, it was a canvas tarp covering something. Harry peeked under the edge of the tarp and saw a car. Peering around, he was startled to see the cabin, not fifty feet away. He caught a whiff of something. Wood smoke. So Ted was at home, probably sitting in front of a cheery fire. Harry crawled under the tarp, lay down, and pulled the special package to him. He lifted the lid and found the big, black wristwatch inside. He took off his Rolex, tucked it in his pocket, and strapped on the plastic digital watch. Checking the time on its red LED display, he got comfortable, and waited for Ted to step outside to use the little outhouse behind the cabin. Then he would confront him. He remembered a dumb joke by his Da.

"Harry, ask me 'What is the essence of comedy?'"

Harry would say, "Da, what is the essence of ..".

"Timing!," Da would shout. And they would both fall down laughing. *Yes, timing is everything*, Harry thought. And waited.

Chapter 38: The Man Who Fell to Earth

November 16, 1975

Luke decided not to shave. In a few minutes, NASA would be launching two astronauts in an Apollo capsule to retrieve him. The three of them would splash down in the Pacific and be picked up by the aircraft carrier *Nimitz*. There'd be lots of photographers onboard so Luke wanted to look presentable. His buzzcut and facial hair had grown out over the months. He trimmed his beard, letting a vacuum cleaner catch the stray floating hairs, until he thought he looked as good as possible. *Not bad*, he thought, checking the results in a small mirror. *Maybe a bit like my Viking ancestors.*

He began prepping the animals for their trip, adding padding he had cut from blankets to the floors of their cages. The gee-forces from slamming back into the atmosphere would be fierce and he wanted to protect them. There was no rush to prep though. Once launched, the rescue crew would be in space within ten minutes but it would take awhile, at least an hour, for them to match orbits and rendezvous with the Soviet space station.

Luke sat at the control panel and flipped comm switches. "Mission Controls NASA and Moscow, Skylab 5 here. Do you read me? Over."

Deke Slayton answered, "NASA Mission Control here. We read you, Skylab 5. Launch in T minus 10 minutes. Over."

"I'll be ready when they arrive. For now, I'll go radio silent and stay out of your hair. Over." Luke finished packing personal items. He looked at his dog-eared photo of Althea. She had already been flown to the carrier *Nimitz* and would meet him on deck after the capsule was hoisted from the Pacific ocean. The press loved photos of them together, the beautiful black woman and blond, blue-eyed farmboy. He just hoped that after months in zero gravity he could stand proud next to her. He slid her photo into a breast pocket, near his heart.

"Skylab 5, Moscow Mission Control here. Do you read me? Over."

"Hello Pyotr. I read you loud and clear. Over."

"Luke, good luck on your flight. I repeat our invitation for you and your dear Doctor to visit us in Moscow soon. The first round is on you but, after that, we will treat you to true Soviet hospitality. I will give you both a tour of our space facilities. No photos please." Luke laughed.

Pyotr went on, "But Luke, I also have something serious to say." He paused. "Sometimes launches have issues, perhaps delays." He paused again. They both knew there was at best only ten days of air left in the space station tanks and no time for NASA to prepare another flight. The Soviet Space Agency was pursuing their own unmanned mission plans. They had made it clear they did not want to expend any more resources on what they considered a flawed American mission. Luke felt lucky they had allowed Pyotr and NASA to stay in touch with him.

"Yes, Pyotr, I am well aware of the risks. All I can do is hope for the best. Is this Russian pessimism versus Yankee optimism?" said Luke.

Pyotr didn't laugh. "No, Luke, just the opposite. I am asking you, if the shit strikes the fan, please don't despair."

"Phew. OK, Pyotr, I promise."

"Also, I am Belarusian, not Russian," said Pyotr.

"Sorry brother. Gotta go. See you on the other side. Over," said Luke. He hung up.

#

Althea sat in the mess hall of the carrier *Nimitz*, with the Captain, some reporters, and a dozen crew members. She tried to ignore the photographers. A TV had been installed for the occasion and they were watching coverage of the rescue launch. Walter Cronkite was the anchorman for the broadcast. His deep voice and measured delivery, as always, provided some comfort in a tense situation.

"T-minus two minutes to launch of the last Saturn 1B rocket," he intoned, "Astronauts Vance Brand and Don Lind will rendezvous their Apollo capsule with the Soviet Salyut 4 station and return to Earth with astronaut Luke Priss. Lieutenant Priss barely escaped the destruction of Skylab from a bomb secretly

194

planted in the station by the infamous 'Math Bomber', who is still at large. In a daring maneuver, Lieutenant Priss took refuge in the Soviet Salyut station."

Cronkite nodded at a signal from his producer. "We go now to NASA Flight Control."

The tall rocket on Launch Pad 39B filled the TV screen. Althea sat with her hands nervously clasped in her lap, squeezing and releasing, as if she could somehow force everything to be OK by sheer force of will. The flight controller's voice crackled over the airwaves.

"T-minus 20 seconds. Ignition will occur at T-3 seconds." Clouds of vapor wafted away from the rocket in the light breeze. The network cut to Mission Control. Deke Slayton stood in the center of the room, arms crossed and jaw clenched, watching the huge wall display. The view returned to Pad 39B.

"T-minus 10, 9, 8, 7, 6, 5, 4, 3…". Yellow flames burst from the rocket engines. The Saturn 1B slowly rose. "We have liftoff!" The rocket cleared the launch tower and soared out over the Atlantic Ocean.

"The Skylab Rescue Mission, or SRM, has launched. It should reach the stranded astronaut in the next hour or so," Walter Cronkite said. Althea took a deep breath and relaxed a bit. She realized she had been holding her shoulders hunched tightly. Chatter between the two astronauts and Flight Control continued in the broadcast.

Then "Houston, we read a pressure drop to engine 2. Over."

Mission Control responded "Copy SRM. We are increasing flow to remaining engines. Maintaining thrust. Over."

The network cameras were tracking the rocket, now high in the atmosphere. The exhaust plumes from the engines seemed to changed shape. Then disappeared.

"Houston, engines have shut down."

"SRM, initiate abort, repeat, initiate abort. Over."

Althea's hands covered her mouth in horror. A new cloud of vapor surrounded the top of the rocket as explosive bolts separated the Apollo capsule from the Saturn 1B. The capsule was topped with a small solid-fueled rocket on a short tower. That rocket fired, yanking the capsule away from the failed Saturn booster and carrying it off to one side. The Saturn 1B fell toward the ocean. Parachutes deployed from the Apollo capsule.

The network returned to Walter Cronkite. "Something has happened to the Saturn 1B rocket. Apparently the engines have failed. Fortunately, the Launch Escape Motor on top of the Command Module pulled it away from the rocket. Parachutes on the capsule are carrying the two astronauts to splashdown in the Atlantic where they will be retrieved. We will bring you more on this story as it develops."

Althea stood up. The Captain of the *Nimitz* looked at her, startled. Cameras flashed as reporters captured her grim expression.

"Captain," she said, "I'll be in my room." He nodded.

Crew members jumped to make a path for her. She carefully locked the door to the small cabin and sat on the edge of the narrow bunk. She bent forward, buried her face in her hands, and sobbed quietly. *No more.* As an Emergency Room doctor, she prided herself on keeping her cool and staying dispassionate. She would do what she could for her patients and then let go. She couldn't seem to do that for Luke. She felt helpless and rocked back and forth, crying quietly. *No more.*

#

Luke sat in the seat in front of the Salyut control panel. He strapped himself down so he wouldn't drift around the room, bumping into things. He needed to think without distractions. He closed his eyes and breathed slowly. His first thought was for Althea. *I am so sorry, darlin'.* Funny, he was alone in space, the only human off the planet, but he was worried about Althea being alone. She had a hard time asking for help, for support. Right now, she was on a ship in the middle of the Pacific, thousands of miles from the Team, Deke Slayton, her parents. He wanted to talk to her so badly and was about to call Mission Control and ask to link to the ship. But he stopped. NASA had their hands full right now, ensuring the safety of the two other astronauts. Luke wasn't going anywhere, he could wait a bit. And what could Luke say to Althea?

Oh, I'll be fine darlin'. Don't you worry.

Luke thought of other explorers in dire situations. Captain Cook, Magellan, Amelia Earhart. All died on their missions. *Way to go on cheering yourself up, idiot..* Luke took a deep breath and let it out slowly. The ball of panic inside him shrank a bit, enough to let him think. He had almost suffocated getting to the Salyut station. *A dress rehearsal for my final act?* But the air would go bad much slower in the big space station than it had in his cozy spacesuit. He would take a while to die. As a test pilot, he had always thought his death would be very quick, happening faster than he could react. He didn't know if he had the guts to die slowly. Luke resolved that, as the days passed and the air ran out and no brilliant rescue plan magically appeared, he would kill all the animals. No reason they should suffer. He would call Althea and say goodbye. Then he would rip out the communications system. He imagined his thinking would get muzzy and stupid at the end and he didn't want to risk messing up a heroic, tragic ending with some blubbering, incoherent call home. He wasn't sure if he would then just let himself suffocate or maybe leave the station without a helmet and die faster in vacuum. Naw, probably the slow way. When Death came for him, Luke wouldn't meet him halfway. *Make the bastard work for it.*

#

"Skylab 5, connecting you to carrier *Nimitz*. Over," said the night shift NASA Comm officer.

"USS *Nimitz* here. Doctor Nespla is online. Over."

Long pause.

Then very quietly, "Luke?"

"Hey darlin'." Both were silent for long seconds. They knew NASA, the Navy, the Soviets, and possibly the networks and press were listening in.

Finally, Althea said, "Damn it. Damn it to hell."

Luke laughed with relief. Anger was good. Anger was really good right now.

"Doesn't it though?" Luke said.

"I mean, who the hell designed this stupid system?" she

said shakily. Luke didn't quite know what to say to that. He could hear the tears behind her voice.

"Althea, are they taking you home?" he asked.

"Yes they are, yes. Flying back to Florida tomorrow."

"Good. Say 'Hi' to Deke, Billie, and the rest of the Team for me. And, darlin', promise me you'll lean on them. And on Harry. And your parents. Will you promise me that?"

"Yes."

"But Althea honey, this isn't my farewell call to you. Not yet. I won't lie to you, I'm in deep trouble. But we're all busting our brains trying to solve this mess."

Silence.

His heart sank. Luke felt like he was losing her, that the love between them was thinning. He couldn't see her or hold her. After he died, their marriage would be a bitter memory for her. Despair and guilt welled up in him. Better if she had never met him. Their mutual dream of humanity spreading out into the Universe, in some kind of naive Star Trekky positive vision, now felt stupid.

Althea said, "Luke, I'll call you after I get back to Mission Control. OK?"

'Luke', not 'flyboy', he thought.

"OK, darlin'. Safe flight," he said.

"You…". He heard her catch herself, about to say the automatic response "You too".

"I'll call you tomorrow. Bye, Luke." She hung up.

#

The scream shocked Luke awake. He gasped and twisted his body, grabbing a handhold. Gregory Peck crowed again. Luke shook his head. He was amazed he had been able to sleep at all last night. He rubbed his eyes. Better feed and water the animals. Maybe that would shut Gregory up. He stopped. Caring for the animals had been a daily routine, one that gave him some comfort. But what was the point now?

Luke used the toilet and washed his face. Gregory

complained the whole time. He went to her cage and opened it. Startled, she fell silent. When he pulled her out, she didn't peck at him. Stroking her feathers, he held her body against his with one hand. With the other, he gripped her neck.

BANG. The station shook.

What the hell? Luke put Gregory back in her cage. He moved to the control panel to check gauges for any leaks or warnings. The Comm system buzzed.

"Skylab 5, Moscow Mission Control calling. Do you read me? Over."

"Pyotr? Yes, I read you loud and clear. The station was just hit by something. I have to go inspect for leaks so...."

"Luke, I am calling to tell you that we have successfully docked Soyuz 20 to the Salyut 4 station."

Luke was confused. "But I thought there were no more manned missions planned."

"That is true. Soyuz 20 is unmanned. It carries some biological samples that we intended to leave in space for three months."

"Intended?" Luke said.

"Yes Luke. Please go open the hatch of the capsule."

That took a minute. Luke entered the station airlock and checked the gauge on the opposite hatch. It showed zero air pressure on the other side. He stuck his head back into the station and shouted toward the microphone, "Zero pressure outside, Pyotr. This isn't a Soviet prank, is it? You guys have a pretty dark sense of humor."

Pyotr laughed. "No Luke, trust me."

Luke returned to the outside hatch and unsealed it. He heard air hissing but it slowed and stopped as the pressure equalized. He swung the door open and saw yet another hatch before him. He twisted handles and opened it. The inside of the capsule, about as cozy as a VW Beetle, was packed tight with racks and containers. Except for the big, beautiful, wonderful, empty seat in the middle.

Luke let the tears well up, tears of gratitude and relief. He finally wiped his nose on his sleeve and returned to the control panel of the station. "Very nice ship, Pyotr."

"It should serve you well, Luke. I managed to convince our Mission Head weeks ago to allow me to install a flight couch, in case NASA's flight failed. Which it sadly did."

"Why didn't you tell me your plan, Pyotr?"

"Because as I said to you yesterday, launches can fail. Even ours. I didn't want to get your hopes up. Now please empty the Soyuz of its experimental cargo and store it neatly in Salyut 4. We may plan a future mission to retrieve that. There should be room for you to load your animals, samples, and possessions in the Soyuz."

Luke said, "Speaking of my animals, the Soyuz docking caught me just in time. I was about to throttle them so they wouldn't have a distressing, slow death."

"I am glad," said Pyotr, "Now that you are returning home, there is no longer a need for you to choke the chicken."

Pyotr found Luke's laughter puzzling.

Chapter 39: The Word for World is Forest

Harry lay on the soft, pine needle-covered ground under the back of Ted's car. The canvas tarp covering the car hid him from view. He checked his watch and did a bit of calculating.

Assuming the FBI left their Butte Montana office right after he had called them from the motel that morning…. *And, boy, were they excited….* the drive time to Thompson Falls would be about three hours and twenty minutes. Helen would get back to the motel shortly before the FBI arrived, open the envelope that Harry had left with her mother, read the note, and know she had to guide the FBI to Ted's cabin. She had the only map that showed every private lot in the forest so her guidance was crucial. Harry checked his watch again. He figured he had at least twenty minutes before Helen and the FBI showed up. Enough time to confront Ted in his cabin.

Harry felt his body trembling and watched his hand shaking in fear. He didn't want to die. He wasn't brave like Luke or Althea. But the image of his father's broken and bloody body was seared in his mind. Harry felt sick with a rage he had carried for too long. He set his fear to one side in a tight little compartment of its own. Harry pulled the special package toward him. He lifted the edge of the tarp.

And saw Helen Wheels knocking on the door of the cabin.

Chapter 40: Childhood's End

Harry's mind raced. He had seconds to act, a moment to come up with a new plan. Helen stood on the tiny porch of the cabin. Harry saw the door open. He couldn't hear Helen but imagined she was asking after her friend Harry Remains. Harry could see the figure beckoning her inside. It was Ted. Ted with a buzzcut but definitely Ted. Harry opened the box he had brought all this way, removed an item, and slapped the lid back on. He grabbed a nearby rock, the size of a brick. Helen was in danger. Harry was surprised at the clarity he felt. Still afraid but moving. *Is this how Heinlein heroes feel*? he wondered.

Harry crawled out from under the tarp and walked to the cabin, the box under one arm, and the rock in his other hand. He dropped to one knee at the steps to the cabin and shoved the rock under the edge of the porch, making as much noise as possible. The door opened. Ted stood there, pointing a pistol at him. To Harry, with adrenaline rushing through him, the muzzle opening looked as big as a barrel. *Barrel*, he thought, a little hysterically, *barrel of a gun. Was that part named by people who had had guns pointed at them?*

Harry stood and brushed off his knees with his free hand. "Hello Ted. Rough ground around here." Let Ted think he had stumbled. Harry believed he had a few minutes before Ted would kill him and Helen. Ted would want to know how Harry had found him.

Ted glanced back into the cabin then stared at Harry. "Step inside," Ted said. Harry obeyed. He saw Helen, wide-eyed, standing in a corner. Her jacket was hanging on a wall hook.

"Put the box on the table and take off your coat. Slowly." Harry did so, hanging it next to Helen's. Her pistol was in his coat pocket. He knew if he reached for it Ted would kill him then Helen. Harry didn't know how to use a gun anyway. *Don't you have to move a safety switch on it first or something?* He thought wildly.

"Sit down," Ted said. Harry sat in the one chair at the table. *Guess Ted doesn't entertain many guests.* Ted waved his gun at Helen. "You, move over here." She did, now standing next to Harry.

Ted looked at them thoughtfully. He moved to their coats, rummaged through pockets while keeping his eyes on them, and found the pistol. He seemed mildly surprised. "If you had this, why didn't you just storm the cabin, gun blazing?" Ted's eyes flicked over Helen. "Because your little friend got here first? What the hell is going on, Remains? Why are you here and not the Feds?"

"Because I wanted to talk to you before I killed you," said Harry. Helen gasped.

Ted smiled. "And what did you want to talk about, Remains?"

"I'll show you. Can I open the box?" Harry said.

Ted shook his head. He moved to the table and pulled the box toward him. He put his hand on the lid and hesitated.

Harry actually smiled. He was surprised at that, given the circumstances. *Liars think everyone lies to them. So mad bombers must think every package might explode when opened?* Harry said, "It's safe, Ted. No bomb inside."

Ted grimaced at him, took the lid off the box, and looked inside. "What the hell is this stuff, Remains?". He pulled a pair of handcuffs out of the box.

"Well, I had thought I might use those to constrain you during our talk," Harry said.

Ted shook his head and gave Harry a what-an-idiot look. He pulled a sheaf of newspaper clippings from the box. "What are these?"

"Articles about the people you've maimed and obituaries of those you've killed. Including Michael Corbin, your first victim back in prison. I thought I'd read them to you and we could discuss real people you've hurt. Not the cold, intellectual idea of 'a species of ape that is destroying the Earth and must be brought down' like your stupid Manifesto says. Real people. Anyway, Corbin is how I found you."

Ted's nostrils flared in anger. "How?"

"Well," Harry said, "I knew you took his wallet with you when you drove away from prison in his truck that day. You then went to a lot of trouble to make a new identity as Carl Frikes but you also still had Corbin's drivers license. I thought you might use that as kind of a back-up, last resort identity if you had to bail out on Carl Frikes. Which you did."

Ted's eyes narrowed. Harry knew that the longer he could keep Ted's interest, the longer Helen and he would live. But when Ted felt he knew enough, he would kill them without hesitation. It was a fine dance, a kind of negotiation, the most important Harry had ever done.

Ted made a decision. "Remains, I think you've gone nuts. So to make me feel safer talking to you, let's try something." He waved his gun at Helen. "Girl, put one end of those handcuffs on your left wrist." Helen stared at him, confused.

"Do it!," Ted shouted. Shaking with fear, Helen could barely close the cuff on her wrist.

"Good," Ted said, "Now, Remains, stand up. Slowly." Harry did. "Both of you, move to the end of the bed frame." They moved. "Girl, pass the other end of the cuffs around that nice heavy metal post on the frame. Good. Remains, put that cuff on your right wrist. Nice and snug." They complied. Ted visibly relaxed. "OK, good. You two aren't going anywhere for now. Probably forever." Ted sat in the chair.

"So, can we sit on the floor? It's awkward crouching like this," Harry said.

Ted laughed. "Sure, get comfortable. You've got a lot of questions to answer. First, how did Corbin's license help you find me?"

"I assumed you would use it to get yourself a new hiding place, some remote place like this, probably buying it on a land contract with minimal official documents needed. I had a crew calling every county clerk in the country until they found a purchase of property by Michael Corbin."

"But I never registered the sale with the County."

"The previous owner did. Guess he didn't want to keep getting the tax bill," said Harry.

Ted sucked through his teeth. "Damn it!"

Harry thought they were nearing the end of the conversation and so probably the end of his and Helen's lives. *Time for the closer.*

"And Ted?"

"What?"

Harry reached for the black watch on his wrist with his free hand, twisted the watch face until it clicked, and carefully kept a tight grip on the edge of the watch.

"There is a bomb under the cabin. I put it there when I came to your door."

#

Luke waited patiently in the Soyuz capsule, strapped into the heavily padded seat and surrounded by cages of chickens and rabbits and racks of samples. The Soviet space program relied heavily on automated systems so Luke would do no piloting and just go along for the ride, like the other animals. Fine with him.

"Soyuz 20, Moscow Ground Control here. Do you read me? Over."

"Yes, Pyotr, I read you loud and clear. Over."

"Luke, your return should commence in ten minutes. Over."

"Thank you, Pyotr. Thanks for everything."

Luke closed his eyes and almost dozed while he listened to technicians chatter in Russian. They went silent. The capsule lurched as clamps released it from the space station.

#

"What!" Ted jumped to his feet and pointed his gun at Harry. Harry showed Ted the watch.

"Dead man switch, Ted. Radio-linked to the bomb. The signal from this is the only thing keeping the bomb from exploding. Shoot me, my thumb comes off the watch, the broadcast signal stops, and the bomb goes off. Shoot Helen and I release the button and the bomb goes off. So sit back down and shut up. Now." Ted slowly sat back down.

"Here's the deal, Ted. Before Helen drove me out here, I called the FBI in Butte. They're on their way here," said Harry. *I wish.*

"Why are you telling me this?" Ted shouted.

"I wasn't planning to. I was going to have a nice talk with you until the Feds showed up. If something went wrong, I was willing to blow us both to bits to stop you from ever hurting anyone else again. But, lucky for you, Ms. Wheels showed up here instead of driving back to town like I asked her to."

"Lucky? What do you mean?"

"I mean you can run away. Maybe the Feds haven't sealed off all the roads around here yet. Who knows?"

Ted stood up, wild-eyed and frantic. Then Harry could see him come to a decision. Ted's face relaxed. *Please, please, please make the right choice*, thought Harry, *You're a rational maniac, right Ted?*

Ted laughed. "Well, I've got two guns now. If they corner me, at least I can take a few Government thugs with me. And if they're busy chasing me cross-country, they won't bother coming to this cabin. So I can take some pleasure thinking of you two idiots sitting here, handcuffed and trapped, with your thumb on the button getting tired. You'll doze off, let it slip, and boom. My bomb in your stupid little casino didn't get you but your own bomb will. How sweet!" He laughed again and picked up a duffle bag. He held it up. "Here's a useful tip you'll never get to use, asshole. Always have a bugout bag ready, in case of unexpected visitors. Bye-bye."

Ted walked out, leaving the door wide open. Walking across the clearing to the car, he turned, smiled, and waved. Then yanked off the canvas tarp, got in and started the car. He eased it slowly down the rutted dirt road toward the highway.

Helen tapped Harry on the shoulder. He turned and saw her looking calmly at him. "Harry, there's not really a bomb, is there? You were bullshitting him, weren't you?"

"Ms. Wheels, there is no bomb under this cabin. I noisily shoved a rock under the porch so, when I mentioned a bomb later, he would remember the noise and find my story more believable." Helen gave a loud sigh of relief.

"The bomb is under the car," Harry said.

"What! How?"

"I was hiding under the car tarp when I saw you walk up to his door. I wedged the bomb into the rear suspension. I couldn't take it to the cabin, not with you in here. I guess I thought that I might need to set off the bomb as a diversion later, I don't know."

Helen smiled at him. "Thank you for rescuing me, Harry. But now what?"

"What do you mean?"

She pointed at his hand holding the dead-man switch. "You can kill him, Harry, just by lifting your thumb. Will you?" She watched his face intently.

Harry stared at the radio-linked switch. He thought of his dead father. He sighed.

"No. I can't. I guess I'm not as tough as I thought I was."

Helen said, "Harry, what kind of range does the signal from that thing have?"

"Range?"

The explosion rocked the cabin, shattering the window. Harry reflexively threw his arm around Helen, trying to shield her. They listened to debris pattering down on the roof.

"So not all that far," Helen said. "Did you bring a key to these handcuffs with you, Harry?"

\#

At first Luke watched the Earth rolling by through the window. As the capsule plummeted down at seventeen thousand miles per hour, it began to bite into the atmosphere, slowing quickly. Luke was pressed into his seat. The animals complained. *Oh you just wait, guys. It's going to get a lot worse than this.* A fiery glow grew outside the window as the energy from the slowing capsule turned the air into superheated plasma. The chatter from Mission Control went silent as the fireball blocked radio waves. Luke concentrated on breathing slow and deep. The pressure on his chest grew and grew. It seemed to go on forever. The animals went quiet. Luke's mind felt like it was being squeezed smaller and smaller, existing only to keep him breathing against the crushing force. But, as he felt himself blacking out, he remembered a quote from Jack London, 'I would rather be a superb meteor, every atom of me in magnificent glow, than a sleepy and permanent planet.' *Screw you, Jack.* Then darkness.

\#

Helen and Harry walked along the dirt road toward the highway. They saw flashing lights up ahead. The wreckage of Ted's car was at the center of a shallow crater, surrounded by knocked-down trees, debris and gore. Harry recognized FBI Agents Roley and Pierce in a crowd of people surrounding the scene. He waved to them. A deputy was running yellow tape around the perimeter. An older woman ran up to them. "Helen!"

"Hi Mom. How did you get here?" said Helen. Her mother hugged her fiercely.

"God, I was so worried about you, going off with him." She glared at Harry. "Right after you two drove off, I just had to open that envelope he left for you. The Math Bomber! The FBI! Well, I called the sheriff right away. He remembered old Ira Turner had sold his cabin recently. We called Ira and by the time he showed up the FBI arrived. Ira led us all here. Are you OK, honey?"

Helen managed to break away from the hug. She took Harry's hand. "I'm fine, Mom. Harry saved my life."

Special Agent Susan Roley came over. "Hello Harry. We obviously have a lot of questions for you. We'll leave our forensics people here to collect evidence. Why don't we go back to the Sheriff's office to take your statements?"

"Hey Roley!" Special Agent Joanne Pierce waved them over to her, standing just outside the yellow tape. She pointed to something laying in the bomb crater. "Another leg in a boot! Now we have a matched set."

Susan rolled her eyes. "Might not be enough to identify the body."

Joanne pointed to something round, up in a tree. "Maybe dental records?"

#

Luke woke up hanging upside down from his seat straps. He waited long minutes. His engineer's mind kept circling around the thought *There has simply got to be a better way to do this.* Finally he heard thumping and scraping as the hatch was opened. Sunlight on snowy ground was blinding. Hands reached in, unbuckled his straps, helped him crawl from the capsule, and lifted him onto a stretcher. Someone threw a rough blanket over him. Luke wanted to collapse in relief but the mission wasn't quite over. He struggled to sit up as technicians pulled animal cages and sample boxes from the capsule.

"Careful with those!" Luke said. They smiled and continued to load the cargo into a truck. Luke knew that, despite his friendship with Pyotr, the Soviets would probably keep all the samples and animals. *We'll be lucky if they share the data with us.* Luke threw off the blanket and struggled to his feet. The techs scolded him in Russian and moved to put him back on the stretcher. A fierce glare from him stopped them. He stumbled to the truck. *And what the hell can I do about it?*

Luke grabbed a random animal cage from the truck and staggered back to the stretcher, collapsed clutching the cage to his belly, and threw the blanket back over himself. He saw one tech turn to another, shrug, and twist a fingertip on his temple. *I'm guessing that's Russian for 'crazy'. So be it. I'm damn well going to return with at least a scrap of my mission.* A shriek came from the cage. *Oh hell, it had to be Gregory, didn't it?*

Chapter Forty One: The Stars My Destination

Harry watched Althea and Luke enter the Grand Bahama funeral parlor. They seemed subdued. Harry wondered if that was entirely due to Howard's death. Instead of sitting together, they took seats on either side of Harry. *Uh oh.*

For an eccentric hermit, Howard knew a lot of people, from industry, government, Las Vegas, and Hollywood. Casino managers alone were a large contingent. The eulogies went on for some time, many of them surprisingly sincere. As visitors filed out, Harry said to Althea and Luke, "We need to have a meeting. I'll drive."

#

A movie projector was set up in Harry's suite. Althea and Luke sat on opposite ends of the couch. Harry could see the tension between them. Althea looked at Harry thoughtfully.

"You seem more relaxed than I've seen you for a long time, Harry."

"Yes, I got rid of a demon haunting me. All better now."

Luke asked, "So why did you bring us here, Harry?"

"I'll get to that in a moment. Right now I'm concerned about you two. With Luke back safe and sound, I thought you guys would be all over each other. What the hell's going on?"

Althea's nostrils flared as she stood. "What's going on? I'll tell you what's going on."

They waited. "I don't know," she said and stood there looking miserable. Luke looked confused but moved to hold her. She batted his hands away. He stayed close to her anyway, looking helpless.

Harry sighed. "I want to apologize." They stared at him.

"You two needed my support and I wasn't there for you. I was obsessed with stopping Ted and forgot about my friends."

Althea said, "And what could you have done, Harry?"

"I could have listened to you, Althea. I don't know if you

shared your fears with anyone else but I think you would have with me."

She gave a tiny nod.

"Now I see that you two are having a hard time," Harry said, "Please, sit down."

They sat closer together, Harry was happy to see.

"We all agreed to Howard's Skylab mission plan because we thought it would be a good first baby step to building a spacefaring civilization, something we three grew up reading stories about and dreaming might someday happen. It turned out to be a mess, almost killing Luke."

Harry pointed at Althea. "So you hated it." Wide-eyed, she gave a slow nod.

"But you didn't think you were allowed to. Not only were you expected by the public to be a smiling astronaut-wife, as an SF fan you were supposed to hold on to the dream of an open, expansive future for humans. But it turns out that space is a really tough place, especially if the missions and the launch systems are badly designed."

Harry gestured to Luke. "And what about you? We all learned that you Just. Don't. Give. Up. Despite everything that's happened to you, I bet you'd be willing to do another mission."

Althea looked stricken. Luke glared at him. "What the hell, Harry?"

"I'm sorry. I'm just saying that we should stop. Stop and think. Our first step was a mess. But we did learn from it. So can we move forward in a way that doesn't tear us up, tear us apart?"

"How Harry?" Althea asked.

"Luke, you're a pilot and now an astronaut. But that doesn't mean you need to put your life and Althea's peace of mind at risk. You're also an engineer. You could pursue The Dream with the Hummingbird project. Build a spaceship that flies as safely and as often as an airplane."

Luke said, "Maybe. If Hughes Aircraft keeps the project going and doesn't squeeze me out. Howard was the big cheerleader for it but now that he's gone, who knows?"

Harry said, "But if we did have a safe spaceship, as reliable as the airplanes we all flew in today to get here, wouldn't that ease all our fears? With flights so cheap you two could have a second honeymoon at an orbiting hotel. How about this? Luke, will you promise never to go to space again unless Althea goes with you?" The idea seemed to startle the two.

Luke turned to Althea and took her hand. "I promise."

She squeezed his hand. "Me too."

Smiling now, she turned to Harry. "A pretty promise, Harry, but we're just a lawyer, a doctor, and a hot-shot pilot. Is the hard reality that The Dream died with Howard?"

He replied, "I think it's time to show you this." He closed the curtains, dimmed the lights, and turned on the movie projector.

Howard faced the camera, smiling. Harry thought he looked vital and focused, with no sign that he would be dead from cancer in mere months.

"Good morning. I am Howard Robard Hughes, Junior and this is my Last Will and Testament, dated July 27, 1975."

He went on to list friends, relatives, charities, ex-wives, and dollar amounts, some large, some insultingly small that he was bequeathing each of them.

"Finally, I hereby create The High Frontier Trust to manage the remainder of my estate. I name three trustees: Luke Priss, Doctor Althea Nespla, and my executor and lawyer Harold Remains. I expect them to devote the wealth of my estate to creating cost effective space travel, promoting the development of space resources for the benefit of mankind, while making sound business decisions to increase the value of the Trust over time."

Howard smiled into the camera, "And I expect the three of them to have fun doing it." He winked. "Over and out."

* End *

Acknowledgements

To my sister Marianne for introducing me to science fiction in elementary school.

To Robert Heinlein for inspiring and mentoring all hard SF writers with his work.

To Freeman Dyson for the alt-Apollo mission idea.

To Gregory Stejskal, retired FBI agent, for his advice and information on how the FBI for-real captured Ted.

To Mitchell Burnside Clapp for creating the Black Horse spaceship concept, artfully presented by me as the Hummingbird.

To real-life people Howard Hughes, Deke Slayton, FBI Agents Pierce and Roley, Walter Cronkite, Pyotr Klimuk, and even mad bomber Ted for appearing in my story. I hope my characterizations didn't mangle their real personalities too much. Except for Ted. Screw him.

To the SF writers whose works provided the titles for my chapters. Read them.

To astronomer Fred Watson's rooster, from whom I stole the name of my chicken protagonist, Gregory Peck.

To Clif, Bethany, Ellen, Brent, and Jennifer, my mates in the Ann Arbor Writers Workshop Spinoff Group for their insightful critiques.

And especially to my wife Cynthia for her loving support of my post-retirement scribble efforts.